EVERCROSSED

ALSO BY

ELIZABETH CHANDLER

Dark Secrets 1

LEGACY OF LIES and DON'T TELL

Dark Secrets 2

NO TIME TO DIE and THE DEEP END OF FEAR

The Back Door of Midnight

a DARK SECRETS novel

EVERCROSSED

A KISSED BY AN ANGEL *novel*

ELIZABETH CHANDLER

SIMON AND SCHUSTER

A **pulse** book

First published in Great Britain in 2011 by Simon & Schuster UK Ltd,
1st Floor, 222 Gray's Inn Road, London WC1X 8HB
A CBS COMPANY

Published in the USA in 2011 by Simon Pulse,
an imprint of Simon & Schuster Children's Division, New York.

alloy**entertainment**
Produced by Alloy Entertainment
151 West 26th Street, New York, NY 10001

A CIP catalogue record for this book
is available from the British Library

ISBN 978-0-85707-355-6

10 9 8 7 6 5 4 3 2

Printed and bound in Great Britain by CPI Cox & Wyman, Reading RG1 8EX

To Puck, my officemate,
who purred through all the chapters

EVERCROSSED

Prologue

AFTER HE AWOKE, HE THOUGHT FOR A LONG TIME.

There was no hope. And when there was no hope, there were two choices: despair or revenge. The cowardly and powerless despaired. He would revenge.

Revenge—the word itself gave him strength.

But he must be careful, clever. There were things he didn't know, things he couldn't remember.

He remembered the words, but not where they came from—some old book. It didn't matter; he made the words his own: "Vengeance is mine."

Elizabeth Chandler

If he hadn't lost his heart, the words would have been inscribed on it:

Vengeance is mine.

Vengeance is mine.

Vengeance is mine.

One

"LISTEN. IT'S SO EERIE."

The night mist, smelling as salty as the ocean, swirled around Ivy and her best friend, Beth. The old-fashioned yard swing on which they sat creaked to a halt.

"Listen," Dhanya said again. "It's moaning."

"Get a grip, Dhanya," Kelsey replied. She was sprawled on a white Adirondack chair between the swing and the cottage doorstep, where Dhanya sat. "Haven't you ever heard a foghorn?"

"Of course I have. But tonight it sounds so sad, like it's—"

"Moaning . . . mourning . . . soughing . . . sighing, wailing, waiting for her lover who will never return from the sea," Beth said, then reached in her pocket and pulled out a small notepad and pen to scribble down the foghorn's contribution to her next romantic epic.

Kelsey threw back her head and hooted. "You haven't changed, Beth. Even carrying around that old clicking pen. Why don't you type on your iPhone?"

"Here?" Beth replied. "Where famous writers have scribbled on paper by the light of hurricane lamps burning whale oil, as rain mercilessly lashed their shingled shacks, and not far from their door the wild surf—"

"All right, all right," Kelsey said, waving an impatient leg at her cousin. "I get it."

Ivy laughed. Beth glanced sideways and laughed with her.

Since their arrival on Cape Cod four days ago, it seemed to Ivy that Beth and Will, Ivy's boyfriend, were continually checking to see how she responded to things. Ivy suspected that she wasn't the only one thinking about Tristan's anniversary at the end of June. Ivy had loved Tristan more than anyone or anything in the world. Her joy with him was like nothing she had ever experienced. His love for her felt like a miracle. But June 25 marked one year from the start of last summer's nightmare, one year from the night that Ivy's stepbrother, Gregory, had tried to murder her and killed Tristan instead.

"Fog is so creepy," Dhanya went on, "the way it slowly invades a place, the way it hides things."

It had been foggy the autumn afternoon that Gregory had died, plunging to his death from a railroad bridge. At the end, his desire to destroy Ivy had been so intense, he'd overlooked his own danger.

Now a menacing rumble caused Beth to glance over her shoulder. "Was that thunder?"

Kelsey sighed. "I wish it would storm and get it over with."

"Where's Will?" Beth asked Ivy, sounding worried.

"Painting," she replied, glancing in the direction of the barn, where Will was staying.

The renovated barn—part of Seabright Inn—was only fifty yards from the girls' cottage. Tonight, with Will as its only occupant and his window facing away from the cottage, the building appeared dark. Across the garden, the lit windows of the main house were yellow smudges in the fog.

"I hate this weather," Kelsey said, pulling on her long auburn hair as if she could straighten it. She tossed it behind her shoulders. "I'm getting a bad case of frizz. So are you, Ivy."

Ivy smiled and shrugged. Her hair was always a yellow tangle.

"I can't believe Aunt Cindy didn't put cable in the cottage," Kelsey continued her complaint. "I'm not going to watch TV in the 'common room' with her hooked rugs

5

and old china and flowers! She can't blame me if I go into Chatham and party."

"It's almost midnight, and you won't be able to see the road in front of your Jeep—not in this fog," Dhanya told her best friend. "Will has cable in the barn," she added.

"If he's painting, we should leave him alone," said Beth.

Pink flashes of lightning lit the western sky. The thunder sounded louder, closer.

Kelsey grimaced. "This kind of night isn't good for anything but a sports bar or a séance."

"A séance, that's a great idea!" Dhanya replied. "I'll get out my Ouija board."

Ivy felt Beth shift uncomfortably in the swing. "Think I'll pass," Beth told them.

"Me, too," Ivy said, seeing her friend's uneasiness. She guessed that for Kelsey and Dhanya, communicating with spirits was a party game, but it wasn't for Beth, who was psychic and last year had often sensed the danger Ivy was in.

"Pass? Why?" Kelsey challenged them. "Are séances too middle school for you Connecticut girls?"

"No. Too real," Beth replied.

Kelsey raised an eyebrow but didn't say anything.

Dhanya rose to her feet. She was pretty and petite, with long, silky hair and exotic eyes that were nearly black. "I'm good at séances and other psychic kinds of stuff. People at school are always asking me to do Tarot readings."

"Yeah," Kelsey said, swinging her long, athletic legs down from the arm of the lawn chair. "Dhanya was the star of my sleepovers." Kelsey walked over to the swing and pulled Ivy to her feet. "Come on. You, too, Beth. Don't be a party pooper," she told her cousin.

When Kelsey and Dhanya had entered the cottage, Ivy turned to Beth. "It'll be okay," she said quietly.

"I haven't told them about last summer, about Tristan or Gregory—or anything else."

Ivy nodded. She could imagine Kelsey's astonishment if they told her that Tristan had come back as an angel to protect her from Gregory and that Beth had been the first to communicate with him. Ivy and Beth would never hear the end of it. "They're just fooling around."

"It doesn't bother you?" Beth searched Ivy's face, her forehead creased with concern.

When they first met, two winters earlier, Ivy had thought Beth looked like a sweet-faced owl. Beth's face was thinner now, and her layers of feathery light brown hair had grown out and been styled in a sleek chin-length cut, but her blue eyes were still as large and round as an owl's, especially when she worried.

Several months back, Ivy had seen through her friend's sales pitch for spending the summer on Cape Cod. Beth and Kelsey's aunt, recently divorced, ran her inn on a tight budget. In exchange for their work, Aunt Cindy, as they all were

7

asked to call her, offered them a modest salary and a place to live just minutes from the ocean, a bay, salt marshes, bike trails . . . According to Beth, it was the perfect way to spend their last summer together before college. But it was a summer away from Connecticut that Beth had most wanted for Ivy, Will, and herself—Ivy knew that. Her best friend was determined to get them away from the dark memories of last summer.

"Are you coming or not?" Kelsey called back to them.

"The more we say no, the more they'll insist," Ivy whispered to Beth. "Just play along."

"Coming," Beth replied to her cousin.

They entered the shingled cottage, which had two rooms on the first floor, a living room and, directly behind it, a kitchen with a large hearth, where Kelsey was waiting for them. Ivy and Beth cleared the kitchen table, while Dhanya retrieved the Ouija board from under her bed upstairs. Kelsey searched the cupboards and drawers for candles.

"Aha!" She held up a package of six dark red tea lights that smelled like cranberry.

"We should use white candles," Beth advised. "White attracts good spirits. I'll get some from the inn."

"No, these will do," Kelsey said stubbornly.

Dhanya set the board and planchette on the table.

"Sit down," Kelsey commanded, while she arranged the candles in a circle around the board.

Ivy gazed across the table at Beth and smiled, hoping to ease the tension she saw in her friend's rigid shoulders. Beth shook her head, then frowned at the board between them.

The three rows of the alphabet, the row of numbers, and at the bottom, the words GOOD BYE were turned so that Dhanya could most easily read them. The word YES was blazoned on the corner close to Ivy, NO on the corner by Beth.

"Try not to set yourselves on fire, girls," Kelsey said, closing the cottage's back door to cut the draft. She lit the votives, then extinguished the lights in the living room and kitchen, and sat down across from Dhanya. "So who are we calling back?" she asked. "Who died recently—someone famous, someone wicked—any good ideas?"

"How about that girl from Providence who was murdered a few months back?" Dhanya suggested.

"Which girl?" Kelsey asked.

"You remember—the one strangled by her old boyfriend. Caitlin? Karen?"

"Corinne, I think." Kelsey nodded her approval of the suggestion. "Love, jealousy, and murder—you can't beat that."

"You should know the person you are contacting," Beth advised. "You should be certain of the name and, most important, be sure that your contact is a benevolent spirit."

9

Kelsey rolled her eyes. "Everyone's an expert."

Beth pressed on: "With a Ouija board, you're doing more than just chatting with a spirit; you're opening a portal for that spirit to enter our world."

Dhanya flicked away the idea with a toss of her hand. "In my experience, you are more successful when you open communication with whatever spirit is available and willing. Please join hands," she instructed, "left on top of right."

Beth reluctantly followed instructions, then Dhanya rolled back her head and chanted, "Wandering spirit, grace us with your presence. You have seen what we cannot see, have heard what we cannot hear. We humbly ask of you—"

"This sounds like church," Kelsey interrupted. "We're going to end up with the Virgin Mary."

"Actually," Beth said, "before starting, we should all say a prayer for our protection."

"A prayer to who, Beth?" Kelsey replied. "That angel statue between your and Ivy's bed?"

"I don't pray to *statues*," Beth responded sharply, then added in a gentler voice, "to whichever angel or guardian you want."

"It's not necessary," Dhanya insisted. "We're sitting in a circle—that will protect us."

Beth pursed her lips and shook her head. When she closed her eyes as if praying, Ivy silently said her own prayer. Ivy told herself that Kelsey's obvious disbelief would prohibit anything beyond the five senses from occurring, but she was starting to have misgivings.

"Place your middle and index fingers on the planchette," Dhanya told them. "Spirit, we are inviting you to join us tonight. We have many questions for you and welcome your insights. Please let us know you are present." To the others she said, "We will wait quietly."

They waited. And waited. Ivy could hear Kelsey tapping her foot under the table.

"All right," Dhanya said. "We will move the planchette in a slow circle around the board. That helps the spirit gather the energy needed to communicate."

They moved the triangular piece in a clockwise motion, skirting the alphabet and numbers.

"Not too fast, Kelsey," Dhanya said.

Around and around they went, with circles as smooth and steady as the foghorn's moan. Suddenly the planchette stopped. It felt as if it had caught on something. Ivy glanced up at the same time as Beth, Dhanya, and Kelsey did. Their eyes met above the board.

"No pushing," Dhanya advised softly. "Let the spirit take over. Let the spirit guide."

The planchette started to move again. It felt strong, as if it were pulling Ivy's fingers with it. Ivy studied Kelsey's and Dhanya's hands, searching for a flexed tendon, or tensed finger—some tiny sign that one of them was moving the planchette. It was making a circle again; it was circling backward, she realized.

Ivy's eyes rose to the faces around her. Kelsey's hazel eyes sparkled, more with surprise than mischief, it seemed. Dhanya's eyes were lowered; she was biting her lip. In the flickering candlelight, Beth looked pale.

The planchette made another counterclockwise circle. And another. Ivy counted the circles—six.

"We have to end this," Beth said, leaning forward.

The planchette moved faster.

"End it," Beth said, her voice rising sharply. Outside it was growing windy—Ivy could hear it in the chimney.

"End it *now*," Beth shouted. "Move it to 'Good Bye.'"

Thunder rumbled.

"Move the planchette to 'Good Bye'!"

But it felt as if some strong, inexorable will wouldn't allow them to. The planchette moved faster, still circling counterclockwise, as if the force would bore a hole through the board. Dhanya's eyes grew wide with fear. Kelsey swore. The tips of Ivy's fingers, where she touched the planchette, felt like they were on fire.

"It's making a portal. We have to—"

Beth's words were interrupted by a clap of thunder and flash of light. The front door banged open and closed. Glass shattered.

Beth's mouth stretched open in a silent scream. Kelsey

rose halfway to her feet, her hands still on the planchette. Dhanya pulled back, cringing in her chair. Ivy saw the three girls frozen in a second flash of blue light.

"Angels! Angels, protect us," she prayed, hoping the prayer was not too late.

Two

KELSEY RUSHED FOR THE WALL SWITCH. THE moment after she flicked on the light, they were plunged into darkness again. Rain beat against the windows. A downdraft through the fireplace brought in a burning smell.

Hand trembling, Dhanya tried to reignite the blown-out tea lights. Kelsey grabbed the lighter from Dhanya and finished the candles.

"Anybody home?" a male voice called.

Ivy breathed a sigh of relief. "Will, we're in here. Our

power's out. What happened?" she asked as he entered the kitchen. "What was that crash?"

"The cat, I think. I was headed here when the storm broke. Just as I reached the cottage, the front door blew open. I rushed in, and Dusty came flying in with me."

The girls picked up the candles and carried them into the living room. The large orange cat cowered in the corner.

"You big wuss!" Kelsey said to Dusty. "Look at the mess you made."

A lamp, several dirty glasses, and a pile of seashells lay on the floor next to the sofa's end table. Kelsey lifted up the lamp and tried to straighten its shade. Will picked up the largest shards of the shattered glass.

"I'll get a broom," Beth said, speaking for the first time since she had shouted at them to end the séance.

"Careful," Ivy warned Will when he tried to pick up the smaller fragments.

He turned to look at her for a moment, his dark hair tousled by the storm, his brown eyes shining softly in the candlelight.

Dhanya sat on the sofa, her hands clenched in her lap. Ivy was tempted to put an arm around her but didn't know if she would welcome it. "The storm's already letting up," Ivy said reassuringly.

Dhanya nodded. Ivy fetched the cat and carried him back to the sofa. He was more than twenty pounds of feline, a Maine coon, with creamy tufts of fur tipping his ears. Ivy scratched Dusty's chin, then buried her fingertips in the lion-like ruff around his neck. Dhanya glanced at the cat, but didn't seem inclined to pet him.

Beth returned with a broom and dustpan, a grocery bag tucked beneath her arm. Will positioned the dustpan and she swept the glass into it. Ivy couldn't see Beth's face, but she saw Will look up and study her for a moment, then reach to where her left hand gripped the broom handle, putting his hand over hers. "Are you okay?"

"Yeah."

The expression on Beth's face must not have been con-vincing, for Will kept his hand on hers. "You're sure?"

"I'm sure," Beth said, pulling her hand higher on the broom shaft and continuing to sweep.

Ivy frowned, annoyed at herself for agreeing to the séance. After months of people watching over her, she had inter-preted Beth's concern as another example of her friend being overly protective. She should have realized that Beth, too, needed protection from last summer's memories and fears.

They had just finished cleaning up when Aunt Cindy arrived in a yellow rain slicker. "Neither rain, nor snow, nor the gloom of night stops Aunt Cindy" was how Beth had once described her favorite aunt. She was in her late thir-ties, petite but strong, with a mane of shoulder-length hair the same fading red as Dusty's.

"I meant to give you these the other day," Aunt Cindy said, opening a carton with three battery-operated camp lanterns. She handed one of them to Will, then eyed the cat. "What's wrong with you, Dusty?"

"The storm spooked him," Ivy answered.

"You've never been afraid of storms before," Aunt Cindy chided her cat. "I think you're faking it. You've discovered a good thing, with four girls here to feed and cuddle you." She turned to Will. "Don't get any ideas. *You've* got your own place."

Will laughed good-naturedly. "And that's where I'm headed."

"Okay, does anyone need anything else?" Aunt Cindy asked.

"Nope," Kelsey replied.

"Then I'll see you all at six thirty tomorrow in the kitchen. You've done a great job this week, but tomorrow, when the weekenders come, you'll get your first experience of having a full inn. Get some sleep."

Will sent Ivy a look that was a sweet, long-distance kiss, then flicked his eyes to Beth, as if checking on her one more time, and followed Aunt Cindy into the rain.

"KELSEY TOLD AUNT CINDY WHAT?" IVY EXCLAIMED the following evening, as she, Beth, and Will nabbed a table at Olivia's, an ice-cream shop in the village of Orleans.

"That she and Dhanya were meeting us here. I told her, if questions were asked, I wasn't covering for them."

"These guys from Chatham," Will said, "how does Kelsey know them?"

"She doesn't," Beth replied. "That's Kelsey for you. Believe me, there's no stopping her—I learned that the hard way during our summers together in middle school."

"Well, she had better come ready to work tomorrow," Will said as they scraped their chairs back on the plank floor. "I'm not picking up the slack."

It had been a long day for them, cleaning up from the storm and keeping pace with the constant stream of incoming guests and their assortment of requests. Kelsey had claimed she wasn't feeling well and had returned to the cottage early, miraculously recovering in time for dinner. Both Beth and Dhanya had headaches, but got through on aspirin and tea.

Ivy had skipped tea for some of Aunt Cindy's very potent coffee—the pot kept in the kitchen, not the more guest-friendly brew served to visitors. She couldn't remember the dreams that had kept her tossing and turning the night before, except that Tristan was in them.

Once seated at the ice-cream shop, Will opened a spiral pad and began to sketch. "Your friend's late."

"No, we're early," Ivy reassured Beth, who had suddenly

gotten nervous about her date and asked Will and Ivy to come along. "You look so pretty."

Beth smoothed her hair self-consciously. Liking print fabrics of all kinds, Beth sometimes looked as though she was dressed in mismatched wallpaper. But tonight, under the guidance of Dhanya, Beth had kept it simple. Her amethyst pendant, which Ivy and Will had given to her on her last birthday, accented the violet hue of her blue eyes.

"So when was the last time you saw this guy?"

"Middle school. His family has a vacation house here. I didn't recognize him Tuesday, when Mom stopped for gas on the way here. I don't think he recognized me either—just Mom—she always looks the same.

"I don't know how he got so tall," Beth went on, "or so gorgeous. It's like one of my characters came to life!"

"So what does he look like?" Ivy asked, scanning the crowd.

"He has dark curly hair—lots of it. A strong jaw. Did I mention he's gorgeous?"

"Several times in the last three days," answered Will.

"Somehow he grew shoulders. I mean, a real chest and shoulders," Beth said, gesturing with her hands.

Ivy smiled. "Sounds as if he could be on the cover of a romance novel."

"Along with the shoulders and chest, does he have a brain?" Will asked.

"Yes. He's going to Tufts University."

"So I don't see why you need us here." Will sounded grumpy.

"Well, it's just that I might not be able to think of anything to say."

Will raised his pencil from the paper and stared at her. "Beth, you've been writing romantic dialogue for years!"

"So what does that have to do with talking to a real guy?" she asked.

"You talk to me all the time. Aren't I a real guy?"

Ivy laughed. "Ignore him, Beth. He doesn't get it."

Will glanced from Ivy to Beth, then laughed along with Ivy. "I guess I don't," he admitted, and flipped to the back of his sketch pad, where he and Beth tried out new ideas. They were creating a graphic novel—Beth writing the story, Will illustrating it—about Ella the Cat Angel and her sidekick, Lacey Lovett, a human angel, battling forces of evil. Ivy's ten-year-old brother, Philip, had requested it.

"So, about this new villain," Will said.

"It's a serpent," Beth told him.

"A serpent." Will nodded. "That's good—kind of biblical."

"A serpent with feet," Beth added.

"Excellent," he said, sketching quickly. "That gives us mobility. I'm exaggerating the head so I have room to draw in a lot of expressions."

Beth and Ivy leaned forward, watching the creature

emerge from Will's deft strokes. "No, the head's big, but not like that," Beth said suddenly. "He has a human face. He has eyes with lids and a human mouth, though it can stretch horribly like a snake's." She slid her amethyst up and down its chain. "And tiny ears," she added. "He hears vibrations through his belly. He can hear emotions as well as words—that's what makes him so dangerous."

Will glanced up from his sketch at the same time as Ivy. It sounded as if Beth was seeing something and describing it, rather than make up a description.

"His eyes are gray," Beth continued, pulling on her pendant.

"I was thinking yellow or amber," Will said, "a color like fire."

"They're gray," she insisted. "I'm sure of it."

"Elizabeth!"

Ivy and Will turned quickly toward a guy with dark curly hair and gray eyes. Although his tone demanded attention, Beth didn't reply until Ivy nudged her.

"Hi, Chase," she said, pushing her hair behind her ear.

"You've brought friends," Chase observed. "Nice."

Will stood up and offered his hand. "Will O'Leary."

"And I'm Ivy."

"My two best friends," Beth said to Chase.

"Nice," he repeated.

Ivy studied Chase, trying to interpret "nice." Was he

stating his approval of Beth's friends, or was he annoyed because she had brought them along? She suspected the latter.

The four of them sat down and a minute of uncomfortable silence followed. Will returned to his sketching, apparently unwilling to contribute anything to Beth's romantic dialogue.

"Beth told us your family has a vacation house here," Ivy began. "How lucky!"

"Here, and the Keys and Jackson Hole," he said. "Water or snow, it doesn't much matter, as long as I'm skiing."

"Yeah, that's how I used to be," Will said.

Ivy blinked with surprise. Will hated snow, and his dream destinations were the Big Apple and Paris.

"Really," said Chase, but he didn't sound too interested.

"But that was before I had my three surgeries."

Ivy knew that the only thing Will had on his medical record was childhood immunizations. Part of her wanted to kick him under the table, remind him to be polite; the other part of her wanted to laugh.

"Oh," Chase responded unenthusiastically.

"The doctors told me I could continue to ski, but if I fell, I might never walk again."

Beth stared at Will. Chase looked as if he didn't know whether to believe him or not.

Ivy shook her head. Will glanced at Ivy, smiling mischievously, and resumed sketching.

"So what beaches and trails do you like best on the Cape?" Ivy asked Chase. "If you come here every summer, you must know them all."

"I love Billingsgate Island. I'm taking Elizabeth there tomorrow."

"You are?" Beth replied with surprise.

"Where's that?" Ivy asked.

"In the bay, about six miles from Rock Harbor. It used to be occupied—had a lighthouse, homes, a school, and a factory—but it washed away years ago. Now the island surfaces only at low tide." He turned to Beth. "We'll kayak there and have a picnic."

"It sounds awesome," she said quietly, "but I have to work."

"On a Saturday?"

She nodded. "Weekends are the busiest time at an inn."

"Can't someone cover for you?" He looked at Ivy, as if she might volunteer.

"Aunt Cindy needs all of us," Ivy told him.

Will glanced up from his sketch. "So what kind of summer job do *you* have, Chase?"

He didn't seem to hear Will. "I was hoping you would surprise me with a fantastic lunch, Elizabeth—something you packed just for us."

Perhaps it was the way he said "Elizabeth" that made Ivy leery, like a guy who thought that by speaking a girl's name he could cast a spell over her.

"You would love the island," he went on. "And there's a sunken boat nearby. At low tide, its old ribs rise out of the water. Very mysterious looking. It will inspire one of your stories."

"I'm really sorry, Chase. How about later in the week?"

"I'm busy," he told her.

"What a shame," Will muttered.

Beth's face revealed her disappointment, but she smiled and nodded. "Oh, well. Thanks for asking."

A waitress approached them and broke into a smile. "Hey, Chase, long time no see. Back for the summer?"

Chase stretched and let one hand fall to rest on Beth's chair. "Back until the wind blows me another way."

Will pursed his lips as if to make a whistling sound, but the "wind" never blew, because Ivy gave him a swift kick. "Double dip, strawberry and chocolate," she said to the waitress. "How about you, Beth?"

The order came quickly, but it turned out to be the longest ice-cream date Ivy had ever endured. One of the things that she loved about Will was that—not counting tonight—he had always been inclusive with her friends and family. When he and Ivy were with others, he enjoyed the people Ivy enjoyed. But Chase was the opposite, the kind of guy who isolated a girl with his attention.

Even so, Beth seemed taken with him, and Ivy did her best to keep Will from expressing his opinion after they left the ice-cream parlor. As soon as Beth climbed in the backseat of Ivy's car, Ivy turned to him. "No comments," she told him quietly. "You're not the one who wants to date him."

"Darn right!" he said, and they both laughed.

When they arrived back at the inn's lot, Ivy and Beth were surprised to see Kelsey's red Jeep. They found Dhanya in the kitchen, munching on saltines. "I asked Kelsey to bring me home," Dhanya explained. "She went back out with the guys."

Beth sat down at the table and pulled three crackers out of the plastic sleeve. "Is your headache making your stomach queasy?"

Dhanya nodded and chewed slowly.

"That's how I felt earlier," Beth said. "Kind of dizzy, too."

"You want me to get Aunt Cindy?" Ivy asked. "She might have something in her medicine cupboard to help you."

"No, she'll want to know where Kelsey is."

Ivy followed Beth and Dhanya up the steep stairs from the kitchen, carrying a tray of crackers and mugs with decaf tea, placing the snacks by their beds. The cottage's second floor was one long room, with the steps rising next to the massive brick chimney in the center of the space. A small bathroom had been built across from the chimney. The four beds were tucked in the four corners of the cottage, beneath the sloping roof. Beth's and Ivy's beds were to the left of the steps, Kelsey's and Dhanya's to the right.

"Feels like home," Dhanya said as she pulled her iPod and earbuds out of her purse and climbed into bed. "Thanks, Ivy." Just before Dhanya slipped in the buds, Ivy caught a snatch of the song from *Aladdin*, and smiled to herself, wondering if Disney was Dhanya's form of retro comfort.

Beth snuggled in her own bed, pulling up a light blanket. June nights were cool on the Cape. Turning on her side, Beth reached toward the chest between her and Ivy, letting her fingers rest on the angel statue. She caught Ivy watching her and smiled a little before closing her eyes.

Ivy lay on her stomach, gazing out the low window between her bed and Beth's. Last night there was a new moon, and tonight the thinnest scrape of silver hung in the sky. The scent of the Cape Cod night—salt and pine—was stronger than the pale shapes surrounding her, making the everyday objects seem less real. The love she had shared with Tristan was like that, stronger than any emotion she experienced in her everyday life, even her feelings for Will. She still ached from its intensity.

While Ivy couldn't admit it to anyone, she doubted she'd ever fully heal. For reasons she didn't understand, her life had been spared last summer; but she had not been spared the longing she felt for Tristan. The way Tristan had made her laugh, the way he had drawn her into his life, the way he had delighted in her music—how would she ever stop yearning for him?

Ivy wiped her wet cheek against her pillow, then turned on her side and reached out to touch the carved stone angel. A long time after, she fell asleep.

Three

THE NEXT MORNING, WHILE IVY, BETH, AND DHANYA dressed for work, Kelsey slept, the sheet pulled over her head, the soles of her feet poking out the other end. The girls agreed that if they didn't get her up, this was going to be a long summer of them working and Kelsey partying. She was dragged out of bed and made it to the inn's kitchen at 6:33.

The girls and Will served breakfast, then cleaned rooms and laundered towels and sheets. By Sunday noon, the weekend guests had checked out and Beth and her aunt had

slipped away to church in Chatham. Beth came back looking pleased with herself. "I found you a piano to practice on,
Ivy! A baby grand!"

"Father John said you are welcome to use the one in
the church," Aunt Cindy explained. "Just call ahead to make
sure someone can unlock the door."

Will smiled at Ivy. "We have a whole summer of Sunday
picnics ahead of us," he said, guessing how eager she was
to be playing again. "We can change our afternoon plans to
an evening hike by Chatham's lighthouse and meet at the
church."

Ivy gave him a grateful hug. They finished work and,
after an early supper, she rushed off with her music books.

It was already sunset inside the timbered and white
interior of St. Peter's, with the sun glowing through the
stained-glass windows that ran along each side of the small
church, coloring the walls crimson and gold. A window
above the altar, pieced together in deep blues and greens,
showed a boat tossed in a storm, with Jesus holding out his
hand, inviting Peter to cross the waves.

Ivy's mother chose churches according to the minister
rather than the core beliefs, so Ivy had attended a variety
of them. She couldn't help but feel at home in this church,
with angels roosting in its small side windows and an angel
guarding a fisherman in the round window above the
entrance.

She warmed up on the piano, playing scales, centering herself with each progression, enjoying the rising and falling tide of notes. Hoping she would find a piano, she had asked her teacher for music to work on over the summer. She began with Chopin, loving the feel of the smooth keys beneath her fingers, happily focused in her effort to learn the first movement of the piano concerto.

An hour later, she stretched and stood up. Walking around the small church, she worked her shoulders. The angle of the sun had changed, and the red and gold in the windows burned like dying embers in the growing dusk of the church. Ivy sat down again and played a medley of Philip's favorite songs. It had been really hard to leave her little brother for the summer. She began to play a song that had become special to her and Philip, "To Where You Are." Philip was sure that it had been written about Tristan. The first time Ivy had heard Philip's young voice singing over Josh Groban's, she had cried.

Was Tristan, as the song said, just "a breath away"? Was he still, somehow, watching over her?

Ivy had always prayed to angels, but those angels were not people whom she had actually known and loved. She glanced around at the stained-glass windows. Catholics prayed to saints as well as angels, and saints had been everyday people. When she called out for Tristan in her dreams, was she praying to him? Or was she simply missing him?

Last summer, when Tristan returned as an angel, he had heard Ivy. And Ivy, once she began to believe again, had heard him whenever he slipped inside her mind. But once she was safe from Gregory, Tristan had left. He had told her he would love her forever, but he could not stay with her. From that time on, she couldn't see his glow or hear his voice in her head. Could he still hear her? Was he even aware of her existence?

"If you can hear me, Tristan, this is for you." She began to play Beethoven's "Moonlight Sonata," the movement she had played for him when they were first together. At the end, she sat still for several minutes, tears running down her face.

"I'm here, Ivy."

She turned. "Will!"

He was sitting in the last pew of the church. She hadn't heard him come in. In the deep twilight of the building, she couldn't see his face. He stood up slowly and walked toward her. She quickly wiped away her tears.

When he reached her, he gazed down at her with such sadness in his eyes, she had to look away. He brushed her cheek gently with his hand. "That was the song you played at the arts festival," he said quietly. "It was Tristan's song."

"Yes."

"I'm sorry that you're still hurting."

She nodded silently, afraid that if she spoke, her voice would shake.

"What would you like me to do?" he asked, his voice breaking with emotion. "Leave? Stay? I can wait outside the church until you are ready, if that would help."

"Stay. Stay, Will. I'm ready to go. Come with me while I return the key to the rectory, then let's take our walk."

Will stayed close to her, walking by her side to the car, but didn't take her hand the way he usually did, didn't touch her at all. He drove silently to the parking lot at Chatham Light.

It's just the anniversary, she wanted to tell him. *It's just the time of year stirring up these memories. Everything will be all right.* But she couldn't say that, because she wasn't sure it was true.

The sky over the ocean was dark blue, the first stars emerging in the east. In the western sky, the last splash of orange was fading fast, leaving the long spit of beach that ran south from the lighthouse painted in mauve. They walked the beach close to the water, carrying their sandals.

"We got an e-mail from Philip," Will said at last. "You, Beth, and me. He wants us to look up his blog."

"His blog!" Ivy replied.

"Hey! Some respect, please! I read it—it's an insightful commentary on summer camp. I just hope the counselor he calls "Tarantula Arms" doesn't hear about it."

Ivy laughed. "I guess the counselor's kind of hairy."

"And very mean, at least to a ten-year-old. He *assigned* the boys their buddies. Philip's buddy threw up on him."

"Oh!"

"That was after the other kids bet the buddy that he couldn't eat four hot dogs in four minutes."

"I see. I guess summer camp is where boys train to be frat brothers."

Will grinned at her, and she slipped her hand in his.

"Philip's group is called the Badgers. He's the best pitcher and hitter of the Badgers."

"Of course he's the best. He's my brother."

Will laughed. "He likes rowing. I can't wait till he comes for vacation—I want to take him kayaking on Pleasant Bay."

Ivy turned to look at Will. His dark hair whipped in the breeze. He had the longest lashes, which softened his intense brown eyes. "If I remember right," she said, "you promised him that you two would dress up as pirates."

"Right, well, maybe he'll forget about that part."

Ivy shook her head, grinning. "Philip doesn't forget that kind of promise. I hope you two don't terrorize girls sunbathing on the beach."

Will laughed and put his arm around her shoulder. They walked on, talking about Philip, then shifting their conversation to some of the weekend's quirky guests.

"The people in the starfish room," Will said, referring to the suite decorated in a scallop and starfish motif. "Was that woman his wife or mother?"

"The only thing I'm sure about is that she wasn't his younger lover."

"Maybe he is *her* younger lover," Will suggested.

Ivy laughed out loud. "Beth's going to be filling up her notebooks with characters."

They found the easy rhythm they had known for nearly eight months, walking and talking together.

Strolling back to Will's car, Ivy gazed up at the light-house, its double beacon turning against the starlit sky. "It's beautiful," she said.

"So are you," Will replied softly, pulling her toward him.

Her arms slipped around him. He lowered his head. She would have known Will's kiss blindfolded—gentle, loving, asking, giving. She knew the curve of his upper lip, the place between his neck and shoulder where she often rested her head, the space between his knuckles that she liked to trace, and the way her hand fit into his. Ivy knew and loved these things, as much as she loved Will's kiss.

But she could not stop thinking of Tristan.

AN HOUR AND A HALF LATER, IVY STOOD ON THE cottage doorstep, watching Will as he whistled his way back to his room in the renovated barn, where he hoped to get in some painting. Needing time and space to think, Ivy walked around to the ocean side of the inn. With just two couples staying on until Monday, the Adirondack chairs on the porch and lawn were empty. Shrubs edged the lawn, then gave way to scrub trees and brush that covered the steep side of the bluff down to sea level. At the end of the yard a vine-covered arbor led to wooden steps, fifty-two of them—Ivy had counted—running down to a narrow boardwalk that connected to a path through grassy dunes.

Halfway down the steps was a landing, a small platform with facing benches built into it. Ivy sat down, facing north. During the day, the view was spectacular, the ocean sweeping in behind a sandy point, making a sparkling inlet where lobstermen and pleasure boaters moored. On a moonless night like tonight, the boundaries of land, water, and sky were nearly indistinguishable; the dunes and beach were so deep, Ivy couldn't hear the waves break. But the ocean was present in the salty tang and damp breeze. It was like that when Ivy thought of Tristan—she couldn't see or hear him, but still, she sensed his closeness.

Ivy swallowed hard. What was wrong with her? She had dated Will much longer than she had known Tristan, so why couldn't she stop thinking of Tristan?

She remembered what Tristan's mother had once said to her: "When you love someone, it's never over. You move on because you have to, but you bring him with you in your heart."

Ivy had thought she'd succeeded in moving on. What pained her even more was that Will thought so too.

Ivy loved Will. But did she love him *enough* if she didn't love him the way she loved Tristan? Maybe her idea of love was too lofty; maybe she expected too much of herself and Will.

Ivy descended to the sand, then walked to the edge of the water, finding release in the ceaseless rush and draw of the sea.

She had no idea how much time had elapsed, but when she finally returned to the cottage, she saw Beth standing on the front step, cell phone in hand. "Ivy! Thank God you're back!"

"Is something wrong?"

"We've got to get to Kelsey before she does something stupid. Stupid*er*," Beth corrected herself, grimacing. "Get your car keys. I've got the address, sort of."

"Where's Dhanya?"

"With Kelsey. And only a little more sober than she is."

"Where's Aunt Cindy?" Ivy asked.

"Out still."

Beth's cell phone rang. "Here we go again." After a moment of listening, she said, "Dhanya, I told you before. Take the keys away from her. Throw them in the ocean if you have to. No, no! It's *not* a good idea for you to drive!"

"Back in a sec," Ivy said.

"Should I get Will?" Beth called after her.

"No, he's painting, and it'll take too long for him to clean up."

Ivy returned with her keys and wallet, and they sprinted to the car.

"Where are we going?" Ivy asked, starting the engine.

"To a road somewhere off Route Twenty-eight."

"Beth, three-quarters of Cape Cod is off Twenty-eight!"

"She said Marsala Road. But I've never heard of it."

Ivy entered it into the GPS, with Orleans as the town, then Brewster, then Harwich. "Nothing's coming up."

"She said they passed a lighthouse. Try Eastham and Chatham—they have lighthouses. Chatham first. My cousin always goes where the money is."

"*Marsala Road*, come on, *Marsala Road*," Ivy said

"Morris Island Road!" Beth exclaimed suddenly. "I bet that was it. She was slurring her words. I think there's a place in Chatham named Morris Island."

Ivy typed it in.

"I have an idea for a new app," Beth added, "one that interprets directions from drunken party girls." She pointed to the highlighted route on the screen. "There it is, south of the lighthouse."

Ivy pulled out of the crushed stone driveway and onto Cockle Shell Road. "I know the way as far as the lighthouse. Will and I walked that beach tonight."

Ivy wound her way through the community. Once they got to Route 28, she pushed the speed limit, glad it was 11:50 p.m. and the weekend crowd had departed.

"I could strangle Kelsey," Beth said. "I could just strangle her."

"Try to get her on her cell."

"I did—I couldn't."

"Then try Dhanya again. We need an address."

As Ivy drove, she thought about Will. He'd be upset with them for not asking for his help. But Ivy couldn't ask one more favor, knowing all that he had already done for her, knowing that while she was kissing him, all she could think of—

"She's not picking up," Beth said.

"Keep trying."

They drove through the commercial edge of Chatham and passed the lighthouse. Beach houses lined both sides of the road, most of their windows dark. "Stage Harbor should be coming up on the right," Beth said, looking at the GPS screen. "There it is. The road we're on goes directly to Morris Island. "

A minute later they entered the island's wooded community. Ivy's headlights showed a narrow, winding road and stripes of trees. "Want me to keep going? It's not that big of a place, just a few streets," she said, glancing at the map. "Maybe we can go slowly and listen for the party."

They rolled down their windows. Ivy slowed to a crawl whenever they saw lights through the trees, and listened intently. The road ended with a pair of driveways. As Ivy turned the car around, Beth tried to call Dhanya again.

"I've got her! Dhanya, listen to me. We're close. What's the address? . . . Well, *ask* somebody! Who the heck is giving the party—they must know where they live!"

Beth turned to Ivy. "Unbelievable! She's trying to find the person whose booze they've been drinking."

Ivy shook her head, and drove slowly down the road they had just scouted. It wasn't going to be a fun ride back to the inn, she thought.

"Ivy, look out!"

Headlights came out of nowhere. The person was driving crazily, as if no one else was on the road. Ivy stepped on the brake, then saw that stopping wouldn't help. She had to evade, but the road was too narrow. She accelerated, trying to get to a driveway and pull in.

"Oh my God!" Beth screamed.

Ivy yanked the wheel hard to the right. One moment she could feel the road under her car, the next, it was gone. Two wheels rose in the air as the car rolled, the world of night and trees turning around her and Beth.

"Beth? Beth?" Dhanya's voice sounded small and far away as the cell phone bounced around the car.

The driver's side slammed into something solid. Steel crumpled inward. Before she could cry out, Ivy's world collapsed into a black hole.

Four

FOR A MOMENT, IVY WAS AWARE OF NOTHING BUT darkness. It felt as if all of the night's weight bore down on her, then, unexpectedly, the pressure eased.

"Beth? Beth, are you okay?"

Her friend's eyes fluttered open.

"Beth. Thank God," Ivy said with relief. "We've got to get out of this car. My side is smashed in. We'll have to use yours, okay?"

Beth gazed at her wordlessly.

"You with me?" Ivy asked, uncertainly.

43

Beth continued to stare at Ivy.

"I'll help you," Ivy said, trying to pull herself up, but she couldn't move. "On second thought, you may need to help me. I'm caught somehow."

Beth looked at Ivy as if she couldn't comprehend what she was seeing.

"What is it?" Ivy asked.

Beth began to shake.

"Beth? Answer me."

But it was as if her friend couldn't hear or understand what she was saying.

"Answer me! Beth, please!"

Beth opened her mouth. She screamed and screamed.

"It's okay, it's okay," Ivy told her, trying to calm her. But Beth started to sob. "We're going to be okay. Oh, angels, help. Tristan, help. Tristan, we need you," Ivy called out.

At last she was free of the thing that restrained her. "All right, now." She touched Beth, then pulled back, surprised. She couldn't feel Beth's shoulder. She reached out again and gazed in disbelief as her own hand passed through her friend's.

Then Ivy began to understand why Beth had screamed, why she was sobbing. Free of her body, Ivy was light, as weightless as a moonbeam and floating steadily upward. Looking down, she saw her body in the mangled car, the airbag deployed, and the metal frame of the windshield bent inward. She saw her head against the crushed frame, blood darkening it.

The only pain Ivy felt was an intense yearning for those she loved. Below her, a night mist enveloped Beth and the twisted car. Along the narrow strip of road, another car raced away. The land and sea merged in darkness.

The longing to say good-bye was all that tethered Ivy to the night below. She spoke the names of those she loved, asking the angels to watch over them: "Philip, Mom, Andrew, Beth, Will, Suzanne . . . Tristan. Tristan."

"My love."

Ivy held still, suspended within a cathedral of starlight. The old world that turned beneath her grew still, as if time had stopped.

"Tristan?"

"My love."

"Tristan!" Ivy closed her eyes, so that his voice would become stronger in her. "Can I really hear you? Is it possible? Oh, Tristan, even in death, I want you near me."

"Even in death, my love."

"Always, Tristan."

"Always, Ivy." A gold shimmer enveloped her.

"You told me I had to move on," Ivy said, half crying for the loss of him, half laughing with the joy of finding him. "You said I was meant to love someone else, but I couldn't."

"Nor could I."

"Every day, every hour, I have held you close in my heart."

"As I held you," he said.

"Don't leave me, Tristan," she begged. "Please don't leave again." She felt his warmth wrap around her. "I need you."

"I'll always be with you, Ivy."

She felt his kiss on her lips. "Don't let go!"

"I promise you, Ivy, I'll always be with you," he said again.

His love reached into every part of her, his pure heat burning within her. Suddenly, she felt her heart beating—beating wildly, like a caged bird, against her ribs.

Then he let her go.

Five

"WHAT ELSE DO YOU REMEMBER?" THE WOMAN police officer asked.

Ivy gazed out the window of the hospital room at the pale yellow clouds of early morning. "That's it. The car—the *vehicle*," she corrected herself, since that was what they were calling it, "came from the other direction straight at us. Braking wouldn't help. He was going too fast. I had to avoid him."

"Him?"

"Or her. Or them. Head-on like that, and in the dark,

all I could see was the headlights." She remembered looking down on a vehicle and assuming it was a car—but the perspective of someone floating above her car and the road on which the accident occurred wouldn't make sense to the police. It barely made sense to Ivy—she *knew* rather than *understood* what had happened.

The moment Ivy had become conscious again, her spirit had felt extraordinarily light, while her body had seemed a heavy and clumsy thing to her. She had clung to the memory of being with Tristan, afraid it would slip through the grasp of her earthbound fingers.

"Do you remember anything about the sound of the vehicle?" the police officer asked.

Jolted out of her thoughts, Ivy stared at the woman blankly until she repeated her question.

"No," Ivy said. "Beth was screaming, telling me to watch out. That's all I remember hearing."

They had already gone over why she and Beth were driving on that road. Ivy knew that both of them had been given toxicology tests.

At that point, the nurse entered her room. Andy's genial face was the first Ivy remembered seeing after arriving at Cape Cod Hospital six hours ago. She couldn't recall anything about the ER, but had been told that Beth, Will, and Aunt Cindy had taken turns staying with her and sleeping on the waiting room sofas, and that her mother was on the way.

"Ivy's had a tough night," he began.

"I'm done," the policewoman said, standing up. "If more questions arise, I'll be in touch. Stay safe."

Andy checked the record of Ivy's vitals signs on the room's computer, and shook his head. "Our own miracle girl! I like starting the work week with a miracle." The nurse was tanned, sandy-haired, in his early forties, Ivy guessed. The lines around his eyes crinkled when he smiled. "Your numbers are good. How are you feeling?"

"Great."

"You wouldn't fake it now, would you?"

"No. Well . . . maybe a little," she admitted. "Is this all I get for breakfast?"

He lifted the lid and saw that the plate, like the tray, was empty. "I guess you're not faking it. You know, if word gets around, we're going to have religious pilgrim types flocking here, wanting to touch your head. I have no idea how that head wound stopped itself from bleeding, or how, given the EMS description of the amount of blood in your car, your hematocrit could be normal. But it is. The doctor said he's seen a case like yours before, but between you and me"— Andy lowered his voice—"the guy's full of it. He just doesn't like to admit that there are some things he and medicine haven't figured out."

Like angels, Ivy thought. *Had Tristan healed her? Had he saved her?*

"You have visitors. Mom and little brother first?" the nurse asked.

"Please."

Andy headed toward the door, then turned back to open a drawer next to Ivy's bed. He set an extra box of tissue on the table top. "You might need this."

"Oh, baby!" her mother said, rushing in with Philip behind her.

Andy was right. A handful of tissues later, Ivy said, "I'm glad you didn't wear your eyeliner, Mom."

"Or lipstick," Philip added. His eyes, green like Ivy's, were now rimmed with red. "Or her cheek stuff. She left it all home."

Maggie and her makeup kit were rarely parted. "I'm sorry I upset you, Mom."

"She even forgot her comb," Philip said. "That's why her hair looks like that."

Maggie patted her head self-consciously. "My mind was all on you, baby. But don't worry, I did think to bring you something to wear while you're here."

Uh-oh, thought Ivy.

"Fortunately, the nightgown and robe I gave you last Christmas looked barely worn."

Mostly because they hadn't been. Ivy's friend Suzanne, who was in Europe for the summer, had suggested that Ivy wear the gown and robe combo to the

50

senior prom—or a Halloween party. Of course, it was nothing compared to the bridesmaid dress that Ivy's mother had chosen for her when Maggie and Andrew were married. *Scarlett O'Hara dropped in a bucket of glitter* was what Ivy thought every time she looked at the wedding photos. But it made her smile, because among several informal photos stuffed in the back of the wedding album was a picture of Tristan, in waiter's garb, launching a tray of fresh vegetables over the bridal party. . . .

"Ivy, are you listening?" her mother asked. "Do you want me to help you get this on?"

"I'll wear just the robe," Ivy replied. Like the gown, it was filmy pink and trimmed with lots of feathery stuff.

"See now? It puts color in your face," her mother said.

Philip played with the feathers for a moment, then unzipped his backpack. "I brought you two things."

"A Yankees cap! Thanks." Ivy put it on. "This is going to make me real popular with the doctors and nurses here among the Red Sox nation."

He held up his second gift, a coin, then dropped it in the palm of her hand. The gold piece, an inch in diameter, had an image of an angel with wings spread, stamped on each side. "It came in the mail."

"Part of a solicitation for a religious charity," her mother explained.

"It's beautiful. Thank you, Philip. I'll keep it right by my bed."

"I forgot—Dad told me to give you a hug. He's in Washington at a conference," Philip added, amusing Ivy by giving her a light hug, the way Andrew would have. Only a few months before, Philip had started calling Andrew "Dad." Her brother was young enough to make that adjustment, especially since he couldn't remember the man who was their father.

"And how is Tarantula Arms?" Ivy asked. "Isn't he going to miss you at camp today?"

"Tomorrow, too," Philip said happily. "We're staying overnight."

"Mom, really, there's no need. I'm fine. Look at me—I'm fine!"

"Well, I'm not," Maggie replied. "And Philip and I have already taken a room at the Seabright."

"Will's taking me kayaking," Philip announced.

"Is he?"

"And he's getting us fishing rods."

"Good."

"And he said he saw an awesome kite shop on Route Twenty-eight."

Ivy smiled and swallowed hard. Philip loved Will, as he had loved Tristan. If she and Will broke up . . . Ivy didn't want to think about it.

"We should let Will visit you now," her mother said. "He's been very upset, Ivy. He saw your car before they towed it. In some ways, I think this was more frightening for him than for you."

"Yes, I can see how it might be," she said. "Would you ask him and Beth to come in?"

"Together?" her mother asked, sounding a little surprised.

"Sure."

As soon as Maggie and Philip left, Beth rushed into the room and threw her arms around Ivy. Then she pulled back. "Am I hurting you?"

Ivy hugged her. "There's nothing to hurt."

Will came in quietly behind Beth. Glancing past Beth, Ivy smiled at him.

"I can't believe you're okay," Beth said, gently touching Ivy just above her temple. "In the car, when I looked over at you . . ." She shuddered. "I wish I could get that picture out of my head. I—I don't see how I could have imagined it."

Ivy looked into Beth's eyes, wanting to know what Beth had seen and longing to tell her what she had experienced. Had Beth, who was psychic, sensed something? Ivy wanted Beth to confirm that Tristan's embrace had been more than a dream, but Beth's eyes were clouded with confusion and worry.

"Beth, you look worse than I do," Ivy observed. "Are you okay?"

"Yeah, sure."

"I don't remember anything from the ER. They checked you over, didn't they?"

Beth nodded. "It's just a minor concussion."

"But a major headache," Will said, speaking at last. "I'm trying to get her to take it easy."

He was standing behind Beth, looking at Ivy over Beth's shoulder. Could he see it in her eyes? Did he guess that, more than ever, she was thinking of Tristan? *Maybe not*, Ivy thought, and reached for Will's hand. He reached back, cradling her hand in both of his. Ivy knew Will's hands by heart, long-fingered and strong, almost always flecked with paint. She loved his hands.

"You scared the heck out of me," Will said, his voice shaking.

"Oh, Will, I'm so sorry."

He moved forward and slipped his arms around her, holding her ever so carefully.

"Hey, I'm not breakable. I think I've proven that," she said, holding him tight.

She started to cry, not knowing all of the reasons why. Will wiped away her tears lovingly, as he always had.

"I'll always be with you," Tristan had said. He had meant it—she felt his promise as if it were inscribed on her heart.

But had Tristan healed her only to send her with his blessing back to Will?

Ivy reached for the tissue box. "Nurse Andy thinks of everything. Help yourselves."

"Don't mind if I do," Beth replied, wiping her cheeks.

She and Ivy blew their noses and honked at the same time, which made all three laugh out loud.

"I guess your mother brought the robe."

They laughed again.

A crisp knock was followed by Andy poking his head through the partially closed door of the hospital room.

"Okay, wonder girl," he said, pushing a wheelchair into the room. "I'm sending home your fans. You're wanted in CT world." He patted the chair.

Ivy hugged Beth and Will once more. "Get some sleep, okay?"

"I'll be back this after—"

"I'll probably be asleep," Ivy interrupted Will. "After you've had some rest, if you want to do me a big favor, entertain Philip."

"If that's what you want," Will replied, looking a little hurt.

"Thank you, Will."

When they had left, Ivy turned to Andy, who was pointing to the wheelchair. "I prefer to walk."

"Sorry, it's against the rules."

"But I feel great!" she insisted. "I could walk and bike for miles."

"Then if no one is looking, I'll let you do wheelies."

Ivy laughed. "Yeah, yeah. Let's roll."

Six

I WILL ALWAYS BE WITH YOU, IVY . . . ALWAYS WITH you . . . I will always—

"Be with you in a minute," Ivy heard a nurse calling to a patient. She quickly opened her eyes, read the time on the hospital clock—4:12 p.m.—then dropped her head in her hands. It was happening again: For months after Tristan had died, each time Ivy awoke from a happy dream of him, she ached as if she was losing him for the first time.

Just now, she had been dreaming, Ivy knew that. *But*

not last night, she thought. Last night had been different—it had felt real.

"Hey, Wonder Girl!"

The door of Ivy's room banged back.

"That's what they're calling you," Kelsey said, entering the room, followed by Dhanya, who was carrying a shopping bag.

"Hi, Ivy." Dhanya's voice was soft and worried-sounding.

"Ohmygod!" Kelsey exclaimed when she saw Ivy's pink robe flung across the wheelchair next to her bed.

"It was a gift from my mother," Ivy replied.

Kelsey held it up and Dhanya's look of concern melted into a suppressed giggle.

Ivy grinned. "There's a matching gown in the closet," she said, swinging her feet over the side of the bed.

"I'll get it," Dhanya offered quickly.

"It feels good to walk," Ivy told her.

"Oh, Ivy, I'm so sorry! I should never have called Beth for a ride. I'm responsible for what happened to you. I feel so bad. You could have been killed. It's my fault. If I hadn't—"

"Wait a minute, listen to me," Ivy interrupted Dhanya. "You were right to call Beth. You and Kelsey"—she paused, forcing Kelsey to meet her eyes and acknowledge she had a major part in this—"are responsible for drinking and getting drunk. But not the accident. You didn't cause the accident. Okay?"

Dhanya nodded, a large tear rolling down her cheek.

"Dhanya, I wish you'd save that for tonight," Kelsey said. "Aunt Cindy put Dhanya and me on probation," Kelsey explained to Ivy, "and scheduled a parent conference on Skype."

She opened the closet, then whistled. "Dhanya, this outdoes your Disney Princess gowns."

Dhanya blushed.

"You've seen the Disney bridal gowns, haven't you, Ivy?" Kelsey asked. "Dhanya doesn't have a boyfriend, but she keeps trying to decide which dress she's going to wear when she gets married."

"Back off, Kelsey," Dhanya said quietly.

Kelsey pulled the gown off its hanger and held it up. "Want to try this on?" she teased her friend.

"No," Dhanya replied crisply. "Why don't you?"

Kelsey pulled off her T-shirt and dropped her shorts— she was wearing her bikini underneath—then slipped the nightgown over her head. Built like Serena Williams, she looked both awesome and funny.

"Let's go to the solarium," Kelsey said. "Put on the robe and we can pretend we're twins."

"Or wear this one," Dhanya said, opening her shopping bag and pulling out Ivy's light green robe.

"Thank you," Ivy replied gratefully, slipping her arms through its sleeves.

Kelsey dug in the pocket of the shorts she had just taken off and retrieved her cell phone. "I'm ready."

Ivy sat in the chair as Dhanya pushed and Kelsey walked beside it wearing her bikini and the filmy gown, waving to people in their rooms, then waving at the staff gathered around the nurses' station as if she was the queen of a homecoming parade. Ivy couldn't help but laugh.

The solarium, past double doors at the end of the hall, was a quiet oasis away from hospital chatter and beeping machinery. Filled with sunlight rather than the cold fluorescence of the medical areas, its wicker chairs, ferns, and pots of red geraniums made Ivy feel as if she was sitting on someone's porch.

"We've got the place to ourselves," Dhanya said. "By the window?"

"Perfect."

Dhanya parked the wheelchair then pulled a small white rocker closer, arranging herself as prettily as a cat. Kelsey stretched out on a curvy wicker lounge and checked her phone.

"So let me fill you in on the guys we've met," Kelsey said to Ivy after a moment of thumb flexing. "Think gorgeous and rich."

"Okay."

"More rich than gorgeous," Dhanya corrected.

Kelsey shrugged. "Their cars are gorgeous. Their boats are."

"If they really have those cars and boats, and weren't telling a few lies, like you were," Dhanya replied.

Kelsey shrugged. "So, I exaggerated a little."

"The party was at a fabulous house," Dhanya told Ivy. "So *somebody* had money." She turned to Kelsey. "But who knows who was who."

Kelsey blew through her lips with disgust. "*I* can tell by talking to them. But you wouldn't talk. You're such a snob, Dhanya! You want money, looks, *and class*. You've been hanging around with your parents too much."

Ivy tried to remember what Beth had told her about Dhanya's parents. Her mother was from a very wealthy Indian family, had come to the U.S. as a graduate student, and fell in love with an American. Her father was . . . a lawyer?

"So I have high standards," Dhanya shot back. "If I can have what I want, why should I settle for less?"

She appealed her question to Ivy; Ivy smiled, remaining discreetly quiet, but mentally awarding Dhanya the "point."

"*Anyway*," Kelsey said, dragging out the word, her eyes shifting from Ivy to the entrance of the solarium, "I know where they all beach now."

"Ivy's not in the market for a boyfriend," Dhanya reminded Kelsey, then turned to see what had distracted her friend.

"I know, but a girl can always look," Kelsey replied,

leaning closer to Ivy, hinting not too subtly that Ivy should turn around.

"What if I don't want to?" Ivy baited her.

"Ivy, c'mon! You're not married yet!" Kelsey sat back in the chaise lounge and raised one knee, providing a nice view of her curvy leg. Ivy wondered who this provocative show was for, but still didn't turn around.

"Hey! Don't be shy," Kelsey called out to the person who had entered the room. "Come on over."

"I was just leaving."

The person who held Kelsey's and Dhanya's attention had a deep voice.

"But you just arrived," Kelsey replied, smiling.

Poor guy, Ivy thought, *probably looking for some peace and quiet.*

"Don't let my outfit scare you off," Kelsey persisted. "It belongs to my roommate." She pointed to Ivy. "If you think this is hot, you ought to see her beachwear!"

"Kelsey!" Ivy spun her chair around, ready to defend herself. But when she looked at the guy, all words slipped away. His intense blue eyes seemed to burn through flirtatious remarks and silly explanations. His gaze was both haunted and disdainful, as if he had experienced and knew something terrible that Ivy and her friends would never understand.

As long as he looked at her, Ivy couldn't look away. His face, shadowed with several days of stubble, was striking rather than handsome. Clean shaven and lit with a smile, it was a face that could break a girl's heart, Ivy thought.

Without saying a word more, he turned his wheelchair and left. Ivy heard Andy's voice in the hall outside the door: "Enough already? Okay, pal."

"I bet that's him," Dhanya half whispered to Kelsey. "The guy they were talking about when we stopped to ask directions to Ivy's room."

"You mean the one they pulled out of the ocean in Chatham?" Kelsey replied.

Dhanya frowned. "I thought he was found unconscious on the sand, close to the water."

"Whatever. Must have been *some* party, probably wilder than ours," Kelsey observed, and turned to Ivy. "He won't tell them what happened or how he got there. He won't even tell them who he is."

"It's not that he won't, he *can't*," Dhanya corrected Kelsey. "He can't remember anything."

"So he says," Kelsey noted.

"What's wrong with him?" Ivy asked.

"Nothing, as far as I'm concerned," Kelsey said. "He's rude, but I can forgive that—what a face!"

Ivy tried again. "I meant why was he hospitalized? Was it for any reason other than amnesia?"

Kelsey looked to Dhanya for the answer. Dhanya shrugged.

"In any case," Kelsey said, "it's obvious that Chatham is the place to be."

"We have our own beach at the inn," Ivy pointed out.

"Ivy, you need to stop thinking about yourself and consider Beth."

"What?" Ivy asked, taken aback.

"You know my cousin—she will come to Chatham only if you and Will come. She needs to find a boyfriend of her own. She's way too attached to you."

Ivy frowned, wondering if there was some truth to that.

Kelsey checked her phone again. "Fat chance!" she said in response to someone's message. "Delete. Delete. Delete. . . . Ready, Dhanya?"

Dhanya stood up and grasped the handles on Ivy's chair.

"I can get myself back," Ivy told her. "I'm going to stay here in the sun for a while."

Dhanya dug in her purse and pulled out a small tube of cocoa butter, handing it to Ivy. "Put it on, close your eyes, and pretend you're at the beach," she said.

Ivy lifted the cap and sniffed. "Mmm. Much better than hospital disinfectant. Thanks."

Kelsey stood up. "I've got to get my shirt and shorts, so I'll drop this gorgeous gown on your bed." She pirouetted and danced out the door.

"Thanks for coming," Ivy called after her.

Dhanya hugged Ivy lightly. "Come home soon," she said, and followed Kelsey out of the solarium.

Ivy rolled her chair to another window, one sheltered by an island of plants. She sat there for a long time, looking out at the trees and buildings surrounding the hospital, thinking about distance. How could she feel as if she'd been kissed by someone who was another world away—and as if she was losing touch with someone close enough to kiss? *Memories are a curse*, Ivy thought. If she had no memory of Tristan, she would be able to love Will the way he deserved to be loved.

After a while, she wheeled back from the window to return to her room. That was when she saw him: the guy with no memory. He had come back to the solarium and was sitting quietly in the far corner. Turning his head, he met her gaze. The way his glance darted away from her, then back again, and the searching look in his eyes told Ivy that he wasn't faking it. He was haunted by what he couldn't recall.

Ivy paused, her chair about ten feet from his. "Remembering can be as painful as not remembering," she said.

His face darkened. "Can it? How would you know?"

In some ways he was right; she couldn't know his pain any more than he could know hers. And there was no point in sharing—he clearly didn't want to.

"Have it your way," she said, and left.

Seven

TUESDAY MORNING, IVY WAS RELEASED FROM THE hospital.

"As soon as I get home, I'm mailing you the rest of your summer clothes," her mother said, while they waited for Andy to bring the discharge papers.

"The thing is, Mom, we don't have much bureau or closet space in the cottage. The only thing I really need is a new pair of sneakers."

The ones she had been wearing were blood soaked, as were the clothes she had worn to the hospital. The ER staff had put them in a bag for Ivy, and before discarding them she had looked at them with astonishment. She believed more than ever that Tristan had helped her. How else could she have made it through such injuries?

"Everything you brought to Cape Cod looks the same, sweetie," her mother argued. "I'll take some of those clothes home to free up space for pretty things."

They spent the next ten minutes discussing clothes, going in circles as endless as her mother's love for ruffles. Finally, Ivy's brother rescued her.

"Philip, where have you been?" Maggie asked when he entered the hospital room.

"You told me to wait outside the door while Ivy changed. You never told me to come back in."

Ivy laughed.

Philip picked up the Yankees cap he had given Ivy and placed it on her head. "I gave away the angel coin I brought for you. Is that okay?"

"Of course," she said. "Lots of people in the hospital could use an angel."

"I told him he could pray to Tristan."

Ivy bit her lip. Philip had never stopped talking about Tristan, believing in him as an angel long before Ivy did; now, his faith in Tristan hit Ivy just as hard as the first time Philip had spoken of him. If she told Philip that she had been with Tristan again, that she had felt Tristan holding her, would Philip—

But no, she didn't want to confuse her little brother.

Andy came in with the discharge papers. "Well, young lady," he said, eyes twinkling, "since you are wearing that cap, I have no choice but to politely ask you to leave."

Ivy laughed and thanked him for his help.

It was noon by the time she arrived back at the inn. With just a few guests, the work for the day was done, and Kelsey and Dhanya were wearing their bikinis. Dhanya threw her towel on the swing and rubbed sunscreen on her legs. Beth, in shorts and a halter top, sat on the cottage steps.

"We're going to Chatham," Kelsey said, shaking her keys.

"Lighthouse Beach?" Ivy asked.

"Even better," Kelsey replied, "a private beach. I was personally invited, and I'm allowing Dhanya to freeload on my hard work at Sunday night's party. You can come too, if you hurry."

"Maybe another time. I have a hot date with my shopaholic mother."

"Well, if Mom supplies the credit card, that's not such a bad date," Kelsey observed.

When she and Dhanya had departed, Beth turned to Ivy. "You're not going with Will?"

"He's kayaking with Philip."

"That's what I meant. I thought you were going too."

"No." Ivy felt defensive about her choice. "Mom's leaving tomorrow. I want to spend some time with her." Ivy sat on the yard swing and beckoned for her friend to do the same. "Beth, there's something I need to ask you. After the accident, when you looked at me, did you think I was dead?"

Beth's eyes locked on to Ivy's. For a moment, she didn't answer. "Why are you asking that?"

"Did you?" Ivy persisted.

"Yes, but I was wrong," Beth said. "Obviously."

"I remember telling you we had to get out of the car. You acted as if you couldn't hear me, and when I tried to reach for you, my hand passed through yours."

Beth didn't take her eyes from Ivy's.

"Then I felt myself floating upward. I remember looking down on you and me, and seeing my body crumpled against the car's frame."

"An out-of-body experience," Beth said, her eyes wide with interest. "People who flatline and are resuscitated sometimes report having them."

Ivy leaned toward her friend. "Did you see anyone resuscitate me?"

Beth shut her eyes for a moment, then rubbed her forehead. "I-I didn't see anyone. I think I blacked out for a few minutes. I remember opening my eyes and seeing a flashing light, and someone leaning over me. I tried to tell them about you, but they told me to stay still. I was being put in an ambulance. I didn't know where you were. They must have been resuscitating you then."

"No . . . no." Ivy laid her hand on her heart, remembering the moment she felt its wild beating. She couldn't keep her voice from trembling. "It was Tristan."

"What?!" Beth exclaimed.

"I think Tristan saved me."

Beth frowned. "You mean because you called to him, he sent the paramedics—"

"No, I mean *Tristan* saved me. I heard him. I felt his arms wrap around me. He kissed me."

"Oh, Ivy," Beth said, resting her hands on Ivy's. "He couldn't have. He fulfilled his mission and left you after you were safe from Gregory. The night Suzanne and I spent with you, just before dawn, he said good-bye. You told me that."

"I'm telling you now he was there for me."

Beth shook her head. "It's how your mind has interpreted the experience. Or perhaps you were given a dream of Tristan to comfort you.

"It was him," Ivy insisted.

"Ivy, don't make it harder for yourself! Tristan is dead and gone."

Ivy pulled her hands away.

"I-I think it's just the anniversary that's affecting you like this," Beth said, in a quieter voice. "It will be easier once it has passed. But right now, be careful what you say to Will. He told me that—well, just don't hurt him, Ivy. This anniversary and the way it is making you think of Tristan is very hard on Will."

Unexpected anger flared up in Ivy. She didn't need Beth to remind her about Will's feelings. As if she didn't already feel like a traitor!

Ivy turned away, feeling the way she did the weeks following Tristan's death, when people were giving her advice about how to get over him, none of them understanding how painful it was to remember—and how painful it was *not* to.

"Ivy," her mother called from the back steps of the inn. "You ready? Beth, come with us—girls' day out! I'd love to buy you something pretty."

"Thank you, no," Beth called back. "My headache's back," she said to Ivy without meeting her eyes, then gave a small shrug and retreated to the cottage.

WHEN IVY RETURNED FROM THE SHOPPING TRIP, during which she had successfully distracted her mother from clothes with a search for vintage Sandwich glass, a familiar ringtone sounded on her phone.

"Hi, Will."

"Ahoy!" It was Philip's voice.

"Why, shiver me timbers!" Ivy replied. "Where are you, Bluebeard?"

"Uh . . ."

There was a discussion at the other end with some squawking seagulls in the background, then Will got on the phone and gave Ivy directions to the beach on Pleasant Bay where he and Philip were boating. "Can you come?"

"Just have to change into my suit," Ivy replied.

Arriving at the beach with towels, a bag of cookies, and a thermos, Ivy spotted Will and Philip next to the long green kayak that Aunt Cindy had lent them. They were building a castle, both of them wearing red pirate bandanas on their heads and strings of bright Mardi Gras beads around their necks. Intent on their digging and piling of sand, neither of them saw her—or the camp of girls who were admiring Will.

Tan, his muscles glistening with sweat as he worked, Will's artist hands quickly shaped ramparts and towers. He looked up suddenly, his deep brown eyes shining with pleasure.

"Why, here's a lass!" he said. "Avast ye, Bluebeard."

Bluebeard looked up. "She's a scallywag."

"Be nice, you scurvy dog," Ivy said to Philip, "or I won't share my chocolate chip booty."

"Chocolate chips? Ahoy, me hearty!" Will responded. "Let me spread that towel for you." He took her bundles from her, and standing close, bent his head, resting his forehead against hers. "It's good to see you," he said softly.

Ivy took off her sunglasses and looked into his eyes.

"Pirates don't do mushy stuff," Philip said.

"Shore leave," Will replied, then kissed Ivy.

They spread the towels next to the castle and shared the cookies. Opening a ziplock bag, Will took out a sketch pad and flipped through to a blank page. Pencil in hand, he worked quickly, easily, his eyes moving from paper to Ivy, paper to Ivy.

"I don't really have to look," he said, smiling. "I've got you memorized."

In five minutes he had a sketch of two pirates with a treasure chest between them, a short Bluebeard lifting up a jeweled goblet, a girl pirate lifting up a robe with a feathery hem and collar. Ivy laughed.

"Do you think Lacey and Ella could meet pirates on one of their angel adventures?" Philip asked.

"I'll have to talk to the author, but I think we can arrange that."

Will moved to a fresh page and started drawing more slowly a cluster of trees to their right, working the pattern of their branches against the deep sweep and curve of the bay. He hummed as he drew. His happiness, his joy in that moment, made Ivy ache.

"Philip, want to take a walk?" she asked.

Her little brother jumped to his feet. "Weigh anchor and hoist the mizzen!" he cried.

"Whoa! Where did you get that line?"

"Will."

Will looked up and smiled. "Don't get lost, matey."

Philip looked left and right, then said to Ivy. "That way!"

She was glad that he pointed left, toward the spit of sand that pushed out into the bay, creating behind its trees a secluded cove. She walked silently, while Philip, still young enough to talk out his fantasies, strutted and gave orders to his pirate crew. He found rubies and doubloons at the edge of the water. From time to time, he raised his spyglass and saw danger on the horizon.

When they had rounded the point, they came upon a deposit of sea stones, shiny-wet and glittering in the late afternoon sun. They knelt down to pick through them.

"Philip," Ivy said, trying to sound casual, "you told someone in the hospital to pray to Tristan. Do you still pray to him?"

"Of course."

"And does he answer?"

"You mean, do I hear him?"

"Yes."

"Not anymore. I stopped hearing him after Gregory died."

Ivy nodded and continued sorting through the stones, telling herself she shouldn't have expected anything else, and it was silly to be disappointed.

Philip rolled a pebble between his fingers, then discarded it. "I hear Lacey."

Ivy glanced up. "You do? You never mentioned that before."

"You never asked."

Ivy sat back on her heels, thinking. She hadn't sensed Lacey's presence in the house—hadn't seen the telltale purple shimmer that indicated the angel was there—so she had assumed that when Tristan said good-bye, Lacey had left too.

Of course, Lacey hadn't liked her; Ivy knew that. Lacey had helped her because Lacey cared about Tristan—was in love with him, Ivy suspected.

"Yo ho ho and a bottle of rum," Philip sang, stirring the wet pebbles and sand with his finger. "The doctors told Mom it's a miracle you didn't die."

"Yes, it seems like a miracle. I prayed to"—she hesitated—"an angel."

Philip looked up at her, as if he suddenly understood. "Did Lacey help you?"

"I think some angel did," Ivy replied.

"Let's ask her," Philip said. "Lacey!" He stood and raised his hands to the sky. "Hey, Lacey, Lacey, Lacey. C'mon, Lacey, you scallywag!"

There was no response. Philip shrugged, then knelt to continue sorting through the stones. "I guess she's busy."

"Well, blow me down, if it isn't the old buccaneer and his scurvy sister!" a husky voice said.

"Lacey!" Philip replied happily.

"Hi, Lacey," Ivy greeted her, trying not to let the hope seep into her voice. If Lacey was still here—

"Long time no see," Lacey replied to Ivy, "which works for me." Her purple shimmer came close to them, as if she were crouching on the sand. "This one's perfect." A smooth round stone appeared to hop into Philip's hand.

"What's up, Philip? I can't stay long this time—got a new gig—an apprentice that doesn't have a clue what he's doing."

Philip nodded. "Just a question: Did you save Ivy's life on Sunday night?"

"Ex*cuse* me?" She moved away from where Philip and Ivy were kneeling and appeared to dance along the edge of the water. Her shimmer was as delicate as a sea mist, the deep purple of a mollusk shell. "Save *Ivy*?"

"Beth and I were in a car accident," Ivy explained.

Lacey came closer, circling Ivy, as if studying her. Ivy felt the gentle pressure of fingers against her temple and knew that Lacey was materializing just the tips of them; by the time Tristan had left, he had been able to do that too.

"I've seen paper cuts bigger than that," Lacey said.

"I know," Ivy replied with surging confidence. "Tristan healed me."

"What?"

"Tristan?" Philip asked, sounding as surprised as Lacey.

"Not possible," the angel said adamantly. "Last time I was with Tristan, he was headed to the Light. He had fulfilled his mission—thanks to me," she added. "By now, he's far beyond all of us, hanging out with Number One Director, I'm sure."

"But I felt his arms around me," Ivy insisted, and recounted the details of the accident. When she described looking down at her body in the crushed car, then rising through the starry night, Lacey's purple mist held perfectly still. For a full thirty seconds after Ivy finished, Lacey was uncharacteristically silent. Ivy thought she might have stopped listening halfway through until Lacey spat out, "*Un*believable. Unbelievable!"

Small stones, one after another, were lifted by an invisible hand and hurled into the water.

"Hey!" Philip cried, "that was my best one!"

"Sorry." The shower of stones stopped. "I just hope you were hallucinating," Lacey said to Ivy, "because if what you're describing really happened, there's going to be serious fallout."

Ivy frowned. "What do you mean?"

"Angels can't go around giving the kiss of life."

The kiss of life, Ivy repeated to herself, recalling how, when Tristan kissed her, she was suddenly aware of her heart beating.

"It's against the rules."

"How do you know?" Ivy asked Lacey.

"How do I know? Look at me. What d'ya see?"

"Fog with an attitude," Ivy replied.

"Oh, yeah, I forgot. Give me a second . . ." Lacey materialized herself, then strutted up and down the shore in her ripped leggings and long tank top. "Like my new hair?" she asked, shaking her head. It was tinged purple, long and straight, with blunt-cut bangs. "I picked up a few more skills since we last had the *pleasure* of working together."

"Wow!" Philip exclaimed, reaching out to touch the angel. "The whole you! You're awesome, Lacey!"

"Thanks, kid." She turned to Ivy. "For three years I've successfully put off my mission by breaking the rules. If I'm not the expert on forbidden acts, who is? I'm telling you—Number One Director does not like his cast members changing the script. There will be repercussions."

"Because Tristan *saved* me?" Ivy argued.

"I guess you weren't listening in Sunday school. Don't you remember the fallen angels story? They wanted to be like God, just like God. It's God's privilege, not ours, to give and take life."

Ivy didn't reply. Would Tristan do something forbidden for her sake?

Lacey's mouth curved in disgust. "Only *you* could get a guy killed, and one year later, put his soul in jeopardy!"

Ivy and Philip watched as the angel's body faded into sand, ocean, and sky. Philip laid his hand on Ivy's arm. "Maybe you just dreamed it."

"Maybe," she replied, but the words rang hollow, even to her.

Eight

ON THE WALK BACK FROM THE COVE, IVY ASKED
Philip not to mention to anyone that Tristan had helped her.

"Not even Will?"

It had upset Will just to hear her playing Tristan's song.
"No, I'll tell him myself in a little while. It's best not to mention Lacey either," she added

Ivy was relieved when Philip and her mother left on
Wednesday morning. Taking off the fitted silk blouse her
mother had picked out for her, she pulled on a tie-dyed T-shirt,
an X-Large that was leftover from a school fund-raiser.

For the first time in her life, Ivy was uneasy around Will. Every time he looked at her, she feared he could read her thoughts—and see Tristan there. She trod carefully around Beth and sensed that Beth was being careful around her too. Kelsey and Dhanya, wrapped up in the guys from Chatham, spent most of their time there, which was fine with Ivy. Her most comfortable companion was Dusty the cat.

On Friday, Will drove Ivy to Hyannis to pick up a rental car, which she would use until the insurance for her totaled car was processed.

"You're so quiet," he said when they stopped at a traffic light. "Are you worried about something?"

"No." Her response sounded short and stiff, but Ivy couldn't think of a single word to add to it. "No," she repeated.

Will turned in his seat to study her.

"Light's green," she told him.

He nodded and drove on. "You know, Ivy, it's natural to be a little nervous about driving again."

"I'm not nervous." She saw the tightening in his jaw and realized Will felt as if his thoughtfulness had been rebuffed. "Because . . . it's daytime," she added lamely. "So, I guess it doesn't bother me—the way it might if it were dark, as it was when the accident happened."

They were silent the rest of the way. Standing together in the hot parking lot, waiting for the rental car, Will rattled his car keys and said, "I'll go with you to your appointment at the hospital, and then maybe we can stop for—"

"Thanks, that's not necessary."

He squinted at her. "You haven't driven since the accident. Suppose a car coming from the opposite direction gets too close to the center line. You don't know how you're going to react."

"I'll be okay, Will."

"What if I follow you as far as the hospital, but not all the way home," he suggested.

Ivy shielded her eyes from the sun and the metallic glare of the cars. "I can handle it."

"Ivy, you were in a really serious accident. There's a reason the specialist wants to check you one more time, and I would like to be there. Okay?" He placed his hands on her shoulders.

Ivy pulled back, then saw the surprise in Will's eyes. Since the night they had come together to fight Gregory, she had never pulled away from his touch. "I'm fine," she insisted.

He shook his head. "You haven't been yourself since the accident. Beth has noticed it too."

Ivy prickled. "What do you and Beth do, spend your time talking about me?"

"Excuse us for caring!"

"I need some space, Will!"

His face paled beneath his suntan. "Space . . . from me?"

She hesitated. "From everyone. We're living in awfully close quarters." She could almost convince herself that this was the problem.

"Fine." He took two steps back from her and held out his arms, as if giving her space. "Fine." Then he turned and strode to his car. He turned to her one last time, but Ivy didn't call him back as he may have expected, and he drove off quickly.

"Ready, Ms. Lyons?" the rental agent asked, arriving with a key. "Got you a new Beetle."

She picked up the shopping bag that she had filled with homemade bread, jam, and cookies—gifts for Andy—then followed the agent across the lot.

An hour later, the doctor told Ivy she would send the test results when they came back, but that everything was looking good. "The folks from EMS are still shaking their heads in amazement," the doctor said. "It's nice to give someone such good news."

Afterward, Ivy took the elevator up to the sixth floor and waited for Andy at the nurses' station.

He emerged from the room next to the one she had occupied, looking perplexed. "Has anyone seen Guy? That boy sure keeps me on my toes."

"Not for a half hour or so," a dark-haired nurse answered.

"Hey, look who it is!" Andy's face broke into a smile. "Back for a follow-up?"

"And to give you this thank-you," Ivy said.

Andy peeked into the shopping bag, then pulled out the bread. Even in its wrapping, they could smell the tangy sweetness of the apple-cranberry loaf. Then he took out the tin of cookies and lifted the lid. "Yum."

"It's all homemade. Aunt Cindy does her own cooking for the Seabright."

"You're going to share, aren't you?" the dark-haired nurse asked Andy.

"Maybe," he replied with a grin.

He and Ivy talked for a few minutes, then she walked to the elevator, contemplating the afternoon ahead of her. She wanted to drive for miles, perhaps to the tip of Cape Cod, and get out on the beach and run. She pressed the elevator's down button three times, then spotted an exit sign and headed for the stairway door. Racing down the steps, Ivy enjoyed the loud smack of her feet against the concrete surface. Holding on to the metal railing, she swung around the corners of each landing, as Philip would have. She didn't see the person crouched on the steps, not until she slammed into him. She tumbled forward and he flung out his arms.

"Whoa!" he exclaimed, pulling her back toward him. It was the guy who had been so unfriendly in the solarium.

Ivy regained her balance, but the guy held on, his eyes as powerful as his hands.

"Let go," she said.

They stood side by side on the step, and after a moment, she took a step higher to even out their height.

"Feeling better, I see," he said dryly.

"And you," she answered lightly, "feeling as antisocial as ever."

His eyes traveled down her, and she became acutely aware of her tight jeans and oversize shirt. Determined not to appear self-conscious, she gazed back at him steadily. He was clean shaven today and wore a pair of tattered jeans, old shoes, and a terry-cloth robe that was about a foot and a half too short for him.

"Nice seeing you—and not talking—again," Ivy said, starting down the steps.

"Do you have a car?"

She turned around, surprised by the question. "Yes. Why?"

"I need a ride."

"A ride now? Where?"

"Not far," he replied casually. "The next town over."

Ivy cocked her head.

"Providence," he said.

"Providence is the next *state* over," Ivy told him.

"Wherever," he replied gruffly. "Just get me out of here."

In the fluorescent light, his bruised skin looked grayish green.

"Sorry," Ivy said. "I don't know what kind of medical problems you have—other than amnesia and—"

"I've never been better." He started down the steps toward her.

"Andy's looking for you."

"To hell with Andy. To hell with all of them!" he exploded.

Ivy stayed calm but moved quickly down the stairs, trying to stay ahead of him without triggering a chase that she was sure to lose. "They'll let you out when you are well."

"I can't wait that long!"

She reached the door marked Level 2 and pushed against it. It didn't budge. She pushed again.

He smirked. "Already tried that. I've tried them all." He walked steadily down the steps toward her. "The only one that opens onto a floor is Level G."

Ivy hurried down the steps, hesitating at the door to Level 1, then continuing past it. The guy quickly closed the gap between them, catching her from behind, turning her toward him and backing her against the wall. "Get out your keys."

"Why do you want to leave?" she asked.

"Hand them over," he demanded.

"You don't even know why," she guessed. "You have no idea *what* you're doing or *where* you're going!"

Releasing her, he took a step back. This was her chance

to get away, but something she'd glimpsed in his eyes held her there.

He sat down slowly on the concrete steps, then dropped his head in his hands.

"What's going on?" Ivy asked in a gentler voice.

He shook his head. "I don't know. I just know I have to get away. Somebody's after me, and I've got to get away."

Ivy moved several steps below him and sat down. She saw that his forearms were badly bruised, as was the side of his head, close to his left ear. A long cut scored his neck, just beneath his jaw. There was more to his story than being found unconscious on a beach or saved from drowning; he'd been beaten up—badly.

If he was in serious trouble, she'd be crazy to get involved. For all she knew, he remembered what had happened to him but didn't want to admit it because he was to blame.

Ivy began to rise, then stopped. What if he *did* have to get away—what if someone *was* hunting him down? All he was asking was for a way to leave the hospital. Ivy's instinct was to help. Then again, when first dealing with Gregory, she had trusted her instincts, and she'd been dead wrong.

"What have they told you about your condition?" she asked.

He shrugged her off. "It doesn't matter."

"Answer my question."

Sighing, he complied. "There was water in my lungs. Obviously I've been beaten up. I have a head injury. The brain scans indicate that the memory loss isn't physical." He glanced away. "They had me talk with a psychiatrist—if it's not physical, it must be mental, right?"

"Possibly," Ivy said, feeling for him, remembering how she blocked out Tristan's death and how the "accident" had come back to her bit by bit in horrifying nightmares.

His eyes met hers. "It's happened to you. That's what you meant the other day, when you said that remembering was as painful as not."

She nodded, wishing she could assure him that things would get better, but her situation was different from his. She'd had Will, Beth, her mom, and Philip's care, and the enduring love of Tristan to get her through. What did he have?

"What's your name?" she asked.

"My memory problem must be contagious," he replied. "How would I know?"

"You said you didn't remember how you ended up hurt. You didn't tell me what you *do* remember."

His smile was more of a smirk. "The hospital staff calls me 'Guy.' 'Guy Unknown' is what they've entered in the computer, which, I guess, is one step better than John Doe."

"What should I call you?"

"What would you normally call someone who pushes

you against the wall and demands your keys? Something stronger than *jerk*, I think." Then he stood up and descended the steps, stopping one step lower than hers, as if he had remembered that she had wanted to look him straight in the eye. "I have to get out of here. It's the one thing I know, the only thing I'm sure of."

His dark blue eyes pleaded with her, and Ivy had to pull her eyes away to think clearly. "You're going to have a hard time getting past a security guard in that bathrobe."

He tugged at the hem. "Andy lent it to me so I wouldn't walk the halls and moon people."

Ivy laughed. "Okay," she said, making up her mind. "Take it off."

"What?"

"Take off the robe," she told him, then tried not to stare at the power in his upper body or the bruises that colored it. "Now turn around. Face away from me."

"Why?"

"We're trading."

When he had turned, she removed her oversize shirt and draped it over his shoulder. "Ready," she said, after putting on the robe.

He turned back, wearing her shirt, grinning at her. She had been right: lit with a smile, his face was the kind to break a girl's heart.

"It'll do," she said. The words *Stonehill High* stretched

across his chest and the shoulder seams were pulled tight, but he was less conspicuous in that than in the short robe.

"If there's no security guard, we'll just walk across the lobby like we're doing nothing wrong," Ivy instructed him. "If we get stopped, I'm the patient and you're the person who has come to pick me up. We tell them that we got tired of waiting for Transportation to bring us a wheelchair— they make you leave in one."

"Right."

Ivy reached in her purse for the rental key. She wondered what Beth and Will would say if she told them about this. Then she wondered if her auto insurance covered carjacking.

"So if someone asks, am I your boyfriend?"

"Brother," Ivy answered quickly.

Guy smiled, as if amused by her answer, then started down the steps. He pushed open the door on the ground level and strode confidently into the lobby. He seemed so at ease, Ivy wondered how much experience he'd had at faking it.

They were halfway across the lobby when someone stopped them.

"Miss, do you need assistance?"

As friendly as the voice had sounded, when Ivy turned around, she saw that the security guard was carefully assessing her and Guy.

"No, not at all."

"Are you a patient?"

"I was." Ivy answered truthfully.

"Do you have discharge papers?"

"Of course." She opened her purse and pulled them out, glad that she had written the hospital directions and her appointment time on her discharge papers. She hoped the guard wouldn't notice the date.

Recognizing the forms, the guard waved aside the papers. To Guy he said, "She should have a wheelchair, and you need to bring the car to the curb to pick her up. Hospital policy."

"Okay," Guy replied. "Stay here, Isabel."

Isabel? She tried not to laugh.

He fetched a wheelchair that had been left by the elevator. As Ivy sat down, the guard received a call on his radio. "What's the patient's description?" the guard asked. "Tall, sandy-colored hair—"

"Hang on, Izzy!"

Guy pushed the chair toward the front door so fast Ivy thought they were going to crash into the plate glass.

"Whoa!" she cried as the glass slid back just in time and they shot through the opening. They flew past another occupied chair, across the concrete plaza, and onto the asphalt. "Wait, wait!" Ivy cried.

"Can't wait. Which way?" Guy shouted back.

She pointed. He ran and pushed like a madman, dodging between two cars, then hanging a left, making her shut her eyes and cling to the chair arms.

"Slow down, you crazy thing!" But she was laughing now and he was, too, as they flew past a long row of cars to the end of the lot.

"The white car!" she yelled. "Brake! Brake!"

He did—and nearly dumped her onto the trunk of the VW.

Breathless, leaping from the chair, Ivy unlocked the car with two clicks. Slipping into the driver's seat, she tossed her release papers and purse in the back. Guy left the wheelchair on a patch of grass and hopped into the car. They drove away, laughing, the windows down and the wind in their hair.

Nine

"ISABEL?" IVY SAID WHEN THEY HAD STOPPED FOR A traffic light. "Is that what I look like to you?"

Guy peeked sideways at her. "It seemed like a good name for a sister."

Ivy drove on. Common sense would dictate that she take Route 28, a road with lots of beach traffic and people around, in case he wasn't trustworthy. Instead, succumbing to instinct—or insanity—she chose Route 6, a highway that ran the spine of Cape Cod and would quickly put distance between them and the hospital.

"So, what's your name?" he asked.

"Ivy."

"Ivy. Izzy—I wasn't too far off. But *Ivy* is better for a girlfriend."

She didn't reply, telling herself that he wasn't flirting, and more important, that she didn't want him to.

"Where are we going, Ivy?"

"I haven't decided. It looks as if Andy cleaned you up pretty well."

"Are you saying I looked raunchy?" he replied, then his demeanor softened. "I don't know what I would have done without Andy."

Ivy sighed. "I feel so guilty! I hope we don't get him in trouble."

There was a long silence.

"Well, nothing we can do about it now," she said, glancing toward Guy. "Those Nikes have seen better days."

He lifted one foot and pulled back the shoe's rubber sole, grinning at her.

"I'm taking the Dennis exit. We're getting you new shoes and a shirt."

"We are? Are you any good at shoplifting?" he asked.

"I'm buying," she replied.

"No," he said quickly.

"Yes," she insisted.

"Ivy, no. I don't want you to do anything more for me."

Was this some kind of pride thing? she wondered. "What are you going to do about it?" she asked aloud. "Open the car door and get out? I'm going sixty."

"Seventy," he corrected.

She glanced at the speedometer and slowed down.

Another long silence followed.

She knew what he needed—his family, friends, and memories—but all she had to offer were things that money could buy.

"Do you remember anything?" she asked. "Like whether you live on Cape Cod or were just visiting?"

"I live here."

His initial moment of hesitation tipped her off. "I see. That's why you thought Providence was the next town over, rather than the capital of Rhode Island."

Guy took a deep breath and let it out, as if she were trying his patience. "It's like this. Some things—names, a person, an object, even a smell—seem familiar, but I don't know how or why. As soon as I try to focus on what seems familiar, it slips away."

"That's hard."

She heard Guy turn in his seat and was aware of him studying her; she kept her eyes on the road.

"Was it like that for you?" he asked.

"Yes—and no. I couldn't recall the crash, but I knew who I was when I woke up. And I knew what I had lost."

"Which was?" he asked.

She didn't answer. "Here's our exit."

Ivy drove a half mile along a two-lane road bordered by a mix of deciduous trees and scrub pine, then turned into a lot serving a small strip of stores, where she and her mother had stopped a few days before. Between the shops of Wicker & Wood and Everything Cranberry was a store that sold sportswear. Ivy parked at the sandy edge of the lot, where the trees provided shade. Pulling the keys out of the ignition, she turned to Guy. "What do you think you'll need to get by for a while?"

"I don't need anything from anyone."

"A shirt, sweatshirt, and shorts," she went on, "socks, shoes, underwear . . . a towel. What else?"

He stared straight ahead, his fists in his lap.

Ivy reached for her purse in the back of the car. "Listen, I know this doesn't solve any of the larger challenges you're facing, but it's a start."

Guy exploded. "My *larger challenges*? You talk like a freaking psychiatrist!"

"Would you prefer that I call them *unsolvable problems*?"

"Wouldn't that be more honest?"

"Only if you think they're unsolvable," she said.

"Next you'll be lecturing me on the twelve-step program. Step one: admit you have a problem."

"That's a good beginning," she replied.

He grimaced.

"Not just the admitting part. It tells us that somehow you know about substance abuse programs. It's a clue."

"A clue telling me what?" he asked incredulously. "That my father was an alcoholic? That my brother—or was it my friends, or was it my mother—did drugs? Maybe I did! Or maybe this clue tells me simply that AA made a presentation at my school and I happened to be listening that day. It tells me nothing!"

Ivy struggled to remain patient. "Obviously, one puzzle piece has no significance in itself. But once you start putting it together with other pieces, it will make a picture. Pay attention when you suddenly come up with a puzzle piece— don't push it off the table in a rage."

She dropped her keys in her purse. "Are you coming?"

"No."

"Don't make such a big deal out of it—you can pay me back later. In the meantime, you can't go without a shirt and decent shoes." She waited thirty seconds longer, then got out of the car.

He poked his head out the window. "Nice outfit," he called to her.

Ivy glanced down—the bathrobe! She started to laugh. "Hey, it's my beach wrap."

Using Will's sizes as a guide, Ivy flipped through the

99

brightly colored T-shirts and cotton shorts. Guy was scared, she thought; anyone who'd leave the hospital—a roof, a bed, and food—when he had no other place to go was very afraid of something. His bouts of anger came from his fear and his hurt pride. If Will were in this situation, would he act this way? She wasn't sure, but Tristan had had that kind of pride.

Ivy added to her list of purchases a large backpack, a pair of cargo pants, sunglasses, and a second towel. At the checkout counter she used her debit card, asking for cash back. Then she stuffed the money, the receipt, and other items in the pack.

Emerging from the store, she walked slowly toward the car, mulling over the situation. When she looked up, she couldn't believe it—Guy was gone. She looked around quickly, as if he might have gotten out of the car to stretch his legs, but he had disappeared. She gazed into the green shade of the woods that bordered the parking lot. His escape route—to where? Guy himself probably had no idea.

He had left her T-shirt on the car seat. *Ridiculous, stupid pride!* Taking a pen from her purse, she wrote the name "Guy" on the backpack, then picked up the pack, and with all her strength, flung it toward the trees. Afterward, she drove to Nauset Light Beach, where she ran through the pounding surf until she was exhausted, wishing her jumbled emotions could drain into the sea.

———

"YOU COULD HAVE CALLED," WILL SAID TWO HOURS later. "You should've had your phone on. You had us worried."

He was working next to the large garden between the cottage and inn, sanding an old bookcase he'd found among Aunt Cindy's stash of furniture. Beth sat nearby in an Adirondack chair, a book opened facedown on the chair's flat arm.

"I told you I was fine," Ivy replied.

"Your appointment was hours ago. I thought something was wrong."

Ivy removed her shoes and shook the sand out of them. "I went to the beach."

Will's mouth held a straight line and the muscles in his forearms shone with sweat as he sanded furiously. Beth looked from him to Ivy, then back to him.

"Why would you assume that something was wrong?" Ivy asked.

"Given your track record, Ivy, why would I assume things were okay?"

She didn't reply.

"If Beth, who wasn't even hospitalized, had gone for a follow-up appointment and arrived home three hours after you expected, wouldn't you have worried?"

"Okay, fine, you win," Ivy said, hoping to end the discussion.

Will looked up from his work, his anger gone, but his deep brown eyes troubled. "I'm not trying to win. I'm just trying to understand what's going on."

"Me too," Ivy replied honestly, and headed into the cottage.

Ten

"BUT YOU LIKED TO KAYAK ON THE RIVER AT HOME,"
Ivy said to Beth at noon on Sunday. With only a few guests
staying past the weekend, they had finished work and were
returning to the cottage, following the stone path through
the garden. "Billingsgate Island sounds so mysterious, rising out of the water at low tide—and that sunken ship!" For
the past week, Beth had been complaining of writer's block.
"They'll inspire you," Ivy added encouragingly.

"I guess," Beth replied without enthusiasm.

"Maybe it's not the kayaking," Ivy said, after a moment

of thought, "but the person you're doing it with. Has something happened since the ice-cream date with Chase? You seemed to really like him then."

Beth shrugged. "He texts me a lot."

"Meaning too much," Ivy concluded. "And you're too nice to tell him to back off."

Beth turned to Ivy.

"You know you're too kindhearted," Ivy said, smiling at her friend. "You don't even swat at flies."

"I might swat this one," Beth said as she entered the cottage.

Ivy retrieved a paperback mystery, one of the many left behind by visitors to the Seabright, and carried it around to the inn's porch. Oceanside, running the length of the inn and wrapping one corner, the porch had its own special light. In the early morning it was an airy room adrift in the marmalade and yellow of the sunrise, but gradually it became as cool and blue as the distant streak of sea. When no guests were around, Ivy liked sitting there. Tilting back in a wooden rocker, her feet up on the porch railing, she gazed past the green edge of Aunt Cindy's yard to the ocean and cloudless sky, her mind drifting.

It's such a great feeling, Ivy. Do you know what it's like to float on a lake, a circle of trees around you, a big blue bowl of sky above you? You're lying on top of the water, sun sparkling at the tips of your fingers and toes.

She had pictured it so many times, floating with Tristan at the center of a sun-spangled lake, that the dream had become as tangible as the real memories she carried of Tristan.

Why had she thought that escaping to Cape Cod would put distance between her and her memories? There was water everywhere, and everywhere that there was water, she thought of Tristan.

Ivy sighed, opened her book, and stared at the words without reading them. A week ago she had awakened in the hospital certain that she had been kissed by Tristan. That had been no *comforting* dream as Beth had suggested; rather, it had made her long all the more for Tristan! And it made painfully clear the difference between what she'd had with Tristan and what she felt for Will. The weekend visitors and full work schedule had helped her and Will get through the last few days, but now that they had time to be together, she had been relieved when he said he was headed into Chatham to shop for art supplies.

"Hey, girl, get off your sweet bum and come running with me," Kelsey called to Ivy, shaking her out of her thoughts.

Kelsey had trotted around the side of the inn and jogged in place for a moment. Her auburn hair was pulled high on her head in a bouncy ponytail.

Ivy smiled at the invitation, which she suspected wasn't real, and shook her head no. "How far do you run?"

"Today I'm doing five miles on the beach, which is like ten on the road, then twenty minutes of hard swimming and an hour of biking. I'm thinking of doing a triathlon in September."

"You're amazing," Ivy replied.

"You don't have to tell her that," Dhanya said, stepping onto the porch, carrying a bowl of frosty-looking blueberries leftover from the inn's breakfast. "Kelsey already thinks it way too often."

"*Knows* it," Kelsey corrected, then adjusted her iPod and took off for the stairway to the beach.

Dhanya sat down. "Berries?" she asked Ivy, holding out the bowl.

"Thanks."

Setting the bowl on a small table between them, Dhanya rocked back and forth for a moment, then put her feet up on the railing, studying them.

"Lavender polish looks good on you," Ivy said.

Dhanya wrinkled her nose. "I'll never have pretty feet. Dancers don't—we abuse our toes."

"Do you do ballet?"

"And modern, and jazz, even tap. I used to do Indian, but my teacher was old and strict—she had this thing about attitude. *Discipline, Dhanya, discipline.*" Dhanya imitated a British-sounding accent, and grimaced. "Want to come with Kelsey and me to Chatham today? Max is having a group of friends over from college."

"Thanks, but I'm headed out to Provincetown with Beth and Will this afternoon."

Dhanya sighed. "You're so lucky—Will's great"

"Mmm," Ivy replied, and changed the subject. "Tell me about Max."

Dhanya rolled her eyes.

"Kelsey said you liked him," Ivy added.

"Kelsey would like me to like him. Somehow she thinks he's perfect for me, which is kind of insulting. She keeps telling me I'm a snob. Do you think so?"

Ivy was surprised by the blunt question. "I think most of us are snobs in one way or another. We just don't see our own prejudices."

"Yes, but some people really are nose-in-the-air types," Dhanya asserted. "I hate that. Especially when they do it to me."

"So, what's Max like?" Ivy asked.

"Rich." Dhanya pointed her toes, then relaxed her ankles. "I need to stop digging my feet in the sand. They're paler than my legs. . . . Max is rich and tacky, into stuff like cigarette boats and gaudy sports cars. He may have lots of money, but he acts so . . . blue collar."

Ivy bit her lip to keep from laughing. Before her mother married Andrew, they had lived in blue-collar Norwalk.

"His father owns a chain of discount clothing stores," Dhanya added.

Ivy cocked her head. "So?"

"Max looks like he buys his clothes from his father. I want someone as rich as Max and as classy as Will."

"Maybe that guy will show up at Max's beach party," Ivy replied, trying to hide her irritation—she didn't need anyone to remind her that Will was a great guy. "Did you date someone you really liked in high school?"

"No, but I have a Facebook boyfriend," Dhanya said. "Of course, it's hard to take a guy from Australia to the senior prom."

After a long silence, Dhanya added, "Thanks for not saying, 'Get real, Dhanya.' Kelsey says I live in la-la land. She says I'm afraid of real guys."

For a moment, Ivy felt bad for Dhanya. "Kelsey has a lot to say about you. Maybe she should focus on herself, and leave you alone for a while."

Dhanya smiled a little, "Yeah. Maybe she should. More berries?"

"No thanks."

Dhanya scooped up the last handful, then picked up the bowl and headed back to the cottage.

Opening her mystery, Ivy read the first chapter—read it twice before she had absorbed enough to go on. But eventually the sea, salty air, and sunny porch faded, and Ivy was creeping with the hero down a dark backstreet of London.

About a half hour later, she felt a hand resting on her shoulder.

"Hey, Will," she said. "Get everything you wanted?"

"Who's Will?"

At the sound of Guy's voice, Ivy spun around, not sure if she felt annoyed or glad about his reappearance. "How did you know where to find me?"

"Your hospital papers. How did you know I'd come back to the parking lot?"

He was wearing the sweatshirt and cargos she had bought him—and his old shoes; the new ones were tied to the backpack.

"I didn't. I was just too mad to go back in the store and return the stuff."

One side of Guy's mouth lifted in a smile. He dropped his backpack on the porch. Seeing a new bedroll attached to it, Ivy hoped he had used her cash rather than shoplifting it.

"Have a seat," she invited.

He shook his head and leaned against the railing facing her. "I'm kind of muddy."

"Where have you been staying?"

He shrugged. "Around."

Ivy closed her book. "Around here?"

"Here and there," he replied elusively.

"Have you eaten anything in the last four days?"

"Yeah," said Guy, "but you don't want to know what."

"Sure I do."

He laughed. Was it the unshaven cheeks, the tousled hair, or the mischief in his eyes? What made his laughter sexy?

"Leftovers," he said. "An assortment of leftovers."

"Yum. Why didn't you come here right away?"

"Because you had already done enough."

"Then why are you here now?"

Guy's face grew serious. There was something mesmerizing about his eyes and the way they seemed to peer into her soul. She had no power to look away.

"Because I'm hungry enough." He turned away from her and gazed out at the water. "Nice view."

"So what will it be," she asked, "breakfast, lunch, or dinner?"

"Whatever you have."

She stood up and held open the door for him. "Come on."

"I'll stay outside."

"No one's here," she said. "Come on in."

"What if *Will* comes home?"

Ivy thought she caught a gleam in Guy's eye. "Then I'll introduce you," she said.

"I feel better out here."

Ivy shook her head. "All right, but if I make you a meal, and come back and find you're gone, I'll be really teed off."

"It's almost worth hiding in the bushes, just to see you

lose it," he replied, grinning. Sitting on the floor of the porch, he rested his back against the wood railing.

Ivy retreated to the kitchen, and after a moment's thought made him a cheese omelet, figuring it would have plenty of protein, then cut a huge slab of Aunt Cindy's home-made bread. She added to the tray an assortment of fruit and a cup of tea, and carried the tray through the parlor, pausing to look at Guy through the screen door. His eyes were closed and his shoulders sagged against the porch balusters. Ivy's heart went out to him—he was exhausted.

"I smell food," he said, opening his eyes.

She pushed open the screen door, debated for a moment where to set the tray, then put it on the floor next to him.

"Thank you," he mumbled, and started eating.

Pushing aside her chair, Ivy sat on the porch floor a few feet away, studying him. He had removed his shoes and pushed up one sleeve to eat. She saw that his feet and ankles were bruised badly, as was his forearm. The fight he'd been in must have been brutal.

"So where are you staying?" Ivy asked.

"We already went over that," he replied.

She nodded. "I thought maybe this time you'd answer."

"Around."

Ivy drummed her fingers against the porch floor and asked herself where she would go if she wanted to sleep outside inconspicuously yet be around enough people to acquire "leftovers." Since he didn't have a car, some place not too far away. "Nickerson State Park," she said aloud.

His face remained a cipher. Having set down his fork, he picked up the mug of tea, holding it with both hands, as if he were warming them. It wasn't warmth Guy needed, Ivy thought, but comfort, kindness. She didn't know how to help him; last time, her comfort and kindness had set him running.

"Have you remembered anything about who you are?"

He took a sip of tea. "No."

"Are there still things that seem vaguely familiar?"

Guy frowned and gazed down at his tea. She wondered if he was choosing his words, deciding what to tell her and what to hold back.

"If anything, it's gotten worse. Now too many things seem familiar to make a pattern that I can understand. And sometimes things are contradictory. One day a smell, like a wood fire, gives me a good feeling; and the next day, that same smell makes me want to run."

"When you went to the park, did you see a sign and follow it, or do you think you may have already known it was there?"

He hesitated.

You can trust me, Ivy wanted to say. Sometimes the hardest thing to do was wait until another person decided to trust you.

"I saw it on a map. I remember general things—such as

motels having free maps in their lobbies. When I saw the size of the park on the map, I knew I could survive there and could hide if they came after me."

Ivy leaned forward. "Who's they?"

"I don't know."

"But it's more than one person?"

"I don't know!" His eyes became a stormy blue. "How am I supposed to know?"

Ivy bit her lip, realizing she had pressed too hard. His eyes, looking more gray than blue now, told her that he had withdrawn into his own thoughts and fears. He ran his finger over the long cut under his jaw. Ivy felt afraid for him, but she knew that telling him that would make him even more skittish of her.

"Here's what I can offer you," she said. "A razor and a shower."

"I don't need either," Guy answered quickly.

"You'll probably feel better. If you let me wash and dry your clothes, you'll be good for a few more days."

He grimaced. "Trying to make me respectable?"

"Yeah, if that's possible."

Guy raised an eyebrow and she laughed.

"You have a lot of research to do," she said. "You want people to feel comfortable talking to you."

"You got a point," he said, smiling. "I'll be quick."

A few minutes later, in exchange for the clothes Guy

had been wearing and the dirty clothes in his backpack, Ivy handed a washcloth and towel through the cottage's bathroom door. She had considered raiding Will's room for shaving supplies and deodorant, but something held her back, and she offered Guy her own instead.

"Oh, I'm going to smell good!" he remarked.

"The laundry room is in the inn, back by the kitchen," she told him, then headed off with her bundle.

While the washer was filling, Ivy searched Guy's pockets to make sure they were empty. She found a sheet taken from her release papers, listing the inn's address and her family's contact information, folded into a tiny square. Ivy wrote her cell phone number on it, then refolded the paper and set it in a bowl on top of the dryer. The other pocket had money in it, which she dug out and placed in the same bowl. When a glint of gold caught her eye, she poured the money back in her hand. Her breath caught in her throat.

A shiny coin stamped with an angel lay in her palm, like a sign from heaven.

Eleven

PHILIP HAD REACHED OUT TO GUY AT THE HOSPITAL, IVY thought on her way back to the cottage, just as she had. Her instincts were right; both she and Philip were meant to find and help Guy. Ivy smiled to herself; maybe they were Guy's "angels."

"I need some clothes," Guy called to Ivy from the second floor of the cottage.

Ivy walked as far as the kitchen. "They take longer to wash than you do," she called from the base of the steps. "That's what the beach towel's for. When you come down, help yourself to anything you want to eat."

She returned to the living room to work on a large puzzle, one of the many Aunt Cindy kept for rainy days at the inn. After clearing the coffee table, she sat on the sofa and studied the box top, which showed a painting of an idyllic New England town and bridge. Sorting through the jigsaw box, she pulled out green pieces with straight edges.

Guy came in a few minutes later, munching an apple. His hair was still wet, darker than its usual streaky gold. Ivy's beach towel hung on him like a low-waisted skirt, leaving little to the imagination about his upper body strength—or his injuries. It took all of her self-discipline not to stare at him.

"Where should I sit?" he asked.

"Wherever you want."

He glanced down at the puzzle box, then sat in an armchair that faced the coffee table, making an L with the sofa. Ivy, having extracted a small pile of green puzzle pieces, handed him the box, hoping the puzzle would take his mind off things. As Guy sorted through the contents, pulling out straight-edged pieces of blue sky, he started to hum off-key, which made Ivy smile.

"Are you laughing at me?" he asked.

She met his bright eyes. "I wouldn't dare . . . What *is* that song?"

"You can't tell?" He grinned at her. "Neither can I."

She tried humming what she had just heard, adjusting the flat notes, then said suddenly, "'If I Loved You.'"

Guy looked up at her, startled.

"It's the title," she explained, and sang the first three lines for him.

He laughed. "Oh, yeah, now I recognize it."

"It's from—" Ivy's hand went up to her mouth as she remembered.

"From what?"

"*Carousel*," she answered softly. Last year, when attempting to communicate with her as an angel, Tristan had played on her piano the first few notes of a song from *Carousel*.

"Do you like musicals?" she asked Guy, pulling herself back to the present.

"I guess I do."

They continued working on the puzzle, Ivy musing over the strange connection between events.

"Here's one of yours," Guy said, suddenly leaning close to her, placing the green piece he had found next to those she had gathered.

Ivy was caught off guard—she couldn't explain it, the feeling that swept through her at that moment. She became acutely aware of Guy, felt his nearness like a kind of heat inside her. Astonished, she sat back quickly. She thought about getting up, putting distance between them. But confusion and pride kept her cemented in place. She touched her cheeks, afraid they had turned a warm pink.

"Got another." He leaned across her.

An overwhelming sense of him passed through her like a wave, making her light-headed. This was crazy! Ivy snapped together two pieces, then added a third.

"I think you forced that last one," Guy observed.

She pulled off the wiggly piece. "I know that!"

Perhaps the crispness of her response made him raise his head to study her. His face was three inches from hers. She tried to pull her eyes away, but couldn't. He lowered his eyes. She felt him staring at her mouth. If it were possible for a gaze to be a kiss—

"Hey, I'm back!"

Ivy knocked over the box full of puzzle pieces. About one thousand four hundred little pieces scattered on the floor. "Oh! Hey, Will," she replied, scooping up pieces as he came through the screen door.

Guy leaned over to pick up the box that had fallen between him and Ivy. Will stopped in his tracks. Glancing down, Ivy realized what Will saw from his perspective: a bare back and broad, muscular shoulders.

"Who are you?" Will asked.

Guy straightened up, rose to his feet, then quickly hiked up his towel. Will continued to stare at him, his eyes noting the injuries. Guy gazed back.

"I *said*, who are you?"

"Guy is the name I go by."

"Guy has just gotten out of the hospital," Ivy explained. "He was on the same floor as me."

"Was he?" Will replied tersely. To Guy he said, "I assume you left the hospital wearing something other than Ivy's towel."

Guy grinned. "Yeah, I left wearing her shirt."

Will didn't seem to find that amusing.

"It's a long story," Ivy said.

"I've got time."

"Guy doesn't have a place to live right now," Ivy explained to Will. "He's been dealing with a lot. I told him he could take a shower here. His clothes are in the wash. It's the least we could do for him."

"Yeah, I can see he's dealing with a lot," Will remarked sarcastically, then set down his packages. Ivy felt bad, knowing he had dropped by the cottage first, excited about what he had bought at the art supply store and wanting to show her.

"The problem is, I can't remember what happened to me," Guy said.

The way Will tilted back his head made it clear he didn't believe Guy.

"Will, he can't remember who he is or where he lives," Ivy added, pleading for understanding.

"That's convenient," Will remarked.

"Not when it rains," Guy replied.

"I heard about you," Will said, "from Kelsey and Dhanya. Funny thing, Ivy didn't mention you at all."

Guy looked from Will to Ivy, then back again.

"And nobody seems to be missing you," Will went on. "I wonder why a nice guy like you hasn't been reported missing by friends or family."

Guy nodded calmly. "It would make you think they're glad to be rid of me."

"It hasn't been that long," Ivy said quickly. "Just since Sunday—a week. Maybe your friends and family think you're away on a trip and they haven't been expecting to see or hear from you."

Will turned to Ivy with a look that said, *You're crazy to buy this story.*

Guy gave her a sardonic smile.

"How did you get to the hospital?" Will asked Guy.

"Some people walking a dog found me unconscious and called an ambulance."

"Found you where?"

"Lighthouse Beach," Guy replied.

"In Chatham? Last Sunday, in Chatham?"

"Monday, really," Guy corrected him. "Just after midnight.

"Must have been one helluva busy night for the EMS!"

Guy frowned. "What do you mean?"

"I sure hope you didn't meet up with another car on Morris Island."

"Will!" Ivy said, recognizing the accusation behind his statement. "That's ridiculous! They never found the car that hit us."

"And they never found out who this guy is," Will responded, "or why he can't remember anything, and why he was lying unconscious a short distance from where your car was totaled." Will paced the room, then stopped and turned toward Guy. "I'm sure you have a good reason for leaving the hospital wearing Ivy's shirt. I'd think it would be a little small for you."

"It was," Guy said.

Ivy recounted the situation, seeing that with each detail she gave, Will was growing angrier.

"Let me get this straight," Will said incredulously. "You helped him sneak out of the hospital before he was released by his doctor—probably still needing medical attention, and before, of course, he paid any bills."

"I followed my instinct," Ivy replied, feeling defensive. "I took a chance on another person. Maybe you should try it sometime!"

She saw the hurt on Will's face.

Guy leaned forward slightly, catching her attention. "You said the laundry room was off the kitchen?"

"Yes."

He nodded and headed out the door.

"Will—Will, I'm sorry," Ivy said. "I see how upset you are. I just . . . felt so bad for him."

Will swallowed hard.

"You remember how terrible it was for me last summer, when I couldn't remember things—when everyone else thought I'd tried to kill myself, when I couldn't explain how I'd gotten to the train station. You were so good to me. You believed in me when nobody else did. You took care of me. Guy has no one to believe in or care for him."

"The difference is," Will said quietly, "I already knew you. I knew the kind of person you were."

Ivy nodded. "Yes, yes, you've got a point. I admit . . . I acted irrationally." She didn't add that, given the chance, she'd do it again.

Will walked over and sat on the sofa next to Ivy. He put his arms around her, pulling her close to him. "Sometimes, Ivy, you scare the hell out of me."

Twelve

"DO YOU THINK GUY WILL COME BACK?" BETH ASKED, a half hour later as she and Ivy walked through the fruit trees along the path to the inn's parking lot.

"I don't know." Ivy looked over her shoulder at the cottage swing, where she had left Guy's backpack. After exchanging apologies with Will, she had checked the laundry room. Guy, his money, the angel coin, and all his wet clothes had disappeared. The red towel had been left on the washer, and the backpack in the cottage.

"He's staying at Nickerson State Park, which is a long walk from here," Ivy told Beth.

"We could take his pack and bedroll to the visitors' center. Maybe they have a lost and found."

Ivy shook her head. "Guy's not the kind to check it out. He pretty much stays out of sight."

Beth looked at Ivy sharply. "Why?"

"Just does."

Beth frowned, but she didn't say anything more.

Ivy was sure that Will had told Beth about his meeting with Guy. Beth had relayed to Ivy Will's excuse for not joining them in Provincetown, claiming he was anxious to work with his new watercolor paper. But Ivy knew how much Will had wanted to see the town, an artists' haven. Despite the apologies, he was still upset.

The hour-long ride to the end of the Cape was uncomfortably quiet. Ivy changed CDs several times, as if she could find the right music to regain the easy connection she usually felt with Beth, and was glad when they finally pulled into a parking space.

Provincetown was as colorful and quirky as advertised. Ivy and Beth strolled in and out of the small shops and galleries that crowded its narrow streets. On the surface it seemed as if things were returning to normal between them, as they pointed out to each other the paintings they liked, the odd pieces of sculpture, and handcrafted jewelry made of mystical sea glass. At about five thirty Ivy and Beth bought two raspberry iced teas and carried them to the breakwater at the end of town. Its black boulders, flat on top, stretched a mile across Provincetown Harbor, making a rocky footpath to Long Point beach on the curling finger-tip of Cape Cod. Just beyond halfway, the point at which most walkers turned back, they sat down on a smooth rock. Behind them were the crescent of Provincetown's low buildings and the tall needle of Pilgrim Monument. Ahead were the lighthouses of Wood End and Long Point.

Ivy played with her straw, then dove into the conversation she felt they couldn't avoid any longer. "I guess Will told you about the fight."

Beth glanced sideways at her. "Yeah."

"I was surprised at Will, the way he acted toward Guy."

"How did you expect him to act?" Beth asked.

Ivy heard the prickliness in her friend's voice. "Understanding. Guy's in a really bad situation."

Beth didn't reply.

"He doesn't know who he is or where he belongs. He tries not to show it but he's scared. You can understand that, can't you?"

After a moment, Beth nodded.

"Guy has no idea what happened to him. Beth, I need a favor. Would you use your psychic gift like you did last year for me, and touch the clothes Guy was wearing when he was found, to see if you could access clues about what happened? Would you help him?"

"Help *him*?" She sounded angry—disdainful—not like Beth.

"Yes, *him*. Beth, you can't automatically adopt Will's view of others."

"I don't," she snapped.

"I'm sorry," Ivy replied, "but in this case, you are blindly accepting what Will says. How can you judge Guy? You haven't even met him."

"How can *you* trust Guy?" Beth countered. "You don't even know his name."

"But I know his . . . heart," Ivy said. "I'm not psychic like you, but I can sense the goodness in him."

"Will told me that you helped Guy sneak out of the hospital—skip out without paying bills, and worse, leave without understanding why he was there. Ivy, he was in a violent fight—Will saw his bruises and the cut along his throat."

Ivy looked away.

"For all you know," Beth continued, "Guy could have killed somebody."

"What?!"

"Ivy, this isn't like you," Beth said, "to turn your back on Will—"

"I'm not turning my back on him!"

"—and take up with some guy who is obviously using

you. I don't know what's going on, but you haven't been yourself since the accident."

Ivy turned to her friend. "I could say the same thing about you."

Beth ran her hand along her gold chain with the amethyst and fingered the stone. Letting out a long breath, Ivy gazed at the sea lapping against the breakwater.

"Ivy, listen to me," Beth said, her voice pleading rather than angry now. "Something is very wrong. I can't shake the feeling that something terrible is about to happen."

"Like what?"

"I don't know." Beth's voice quivered. "But you must be careful. This is no time to trust strangers."

Ivy laid her hands gently on her friend's. "I know what I'm doing. It's time for you to trust *me*."

WHEN THEY ARRIVED HOME, IVY SAW THAT GUY'S backpack and bedroll were gone. Beth regarded the empty swing with a look of apprehension and peered through the screen door before entering the cottage, as if Guy might be waiting inside.

Following her in, Ivy was surprised to find Will there, sitting on the sofa, working the puzzle. "Hey, Will."

"Hey. Have a good time?" he asked.

"Yeah! The art is awesome," Ivy replied, hoping to sound upbeat and easy with him. "You'd love it there."

Will studied her, as if trying to tell whether things were "right" between them, then said, "There's no way you can see it all in one trip, so maybe you'll want to go a second time with me. How about it?"

"Of course!" Ivy sat in a chair facing the coffee table. "And this time, with plenty of cash. I saw about ten sets of earrings and an armful of bracelets I liked. I could do all my Christmas shopping there." She leaned forward and pushed a puzzle piece into place.

"Beth, come sit down," Will invited. "I have an idea I wanted to talk over with both of you."

Beth had reached the kitchen and turned back reluctantly.

"I've been thinking about next Sunday," Will said as Beth perched on the edge of the sofa. "Tristan's anniversary, and how to honor him. They allow bonfires at the National Seashore. And there's a beach called Race Point, which seems right for him. What do you think?"

Ivy, knowing how hard Will was trying, felt tears rising in her. "It's a great idea."

"I was thinking of picking up the permit Tuesday afternoon at the visitors' center." Will looked hopefully at Ivy. "How about that and dinner in Provincetown?"

She smiled at him. "Perfect."

Beth rose silently and returned to the kitchen.

Will turned and gazed after her. "Beth, are you okay?"

"Fine," she called back.

Ivy leaned close to Will. "Something's really bothering her."

"I think it's the anniversary," Will said, reaching for Ivy's hand. "She went through a lot with us. You can't just erase memories like that. Things will be easier for all of us after the twenty-fifth."

Ivy looked down at her hand resting in Will's and nodded silently, wishing she could believe that the way he did.

Thirteen

LATE MONDAY MORNING, SPLASHING THROUGH A puddle in the inn's lot, wondering whether Guy had found shelter during a late-night storm, Ivy threw a bag with a beach towel and music books into the backseat of the Beetle.

"Hey, just in time!"

Ivy jumped at the sound of Guy's voice.

"You sure are easy to sneak up on," Guy observed, emerging from the shrubs surrounding the inn's parking lot. "What were you thinking about?"

"Music," she lied—no point in feeding his ego. "I'm headed to practice."

"What direction is that?" Guy asked. His clothes were damp and wrinkled, his backpack slung over his shoulder.

"Chatham. I use the piano at a village church."

"Can I get a ride that far?"

She double clicked her key. "Door's open. Where're you going?" she asked, as he stowed his backpack in the rear seat.

"Lighthouse Beach."

"Have you remembered something?"

"No," he replied. "I was hoping I might if I saw the place."

Ivy thought about offering to go with him, but she had come to think of Guy as a cat, a creature who comes to others only when he's ready.

Guy was wearing his old shoes again. As Ivy pulled out of the lot, she glanced through her rearview mirror at the new shoes, still tied to his pack. "Did I get the wrong size?"

He followed her eyes. "Yup. But they make a nice souvenir."

"We can exchange them for a pair that fit," she said.

"We could, but that's a lot of trouble. And if you'd like to have them back," he added with a sly smile," I have a hunch they'll fit Will."

"If you'd come into the store with me," she replied brusquely, "I wouldn't have had to guess your size."

They didn't speak again till she reached Route 28.

"So . . . if you practice music during the summer, you must be pretty serious about it," he said.

"I am."

He twisted himself around in his seat to reach the books. His arm brushed hers, his body hovering close in the small car. For a moment Ivy felt dizzy, overwhelmed by a powerful sense of his presence. He grabbed a music book and turned forward again in his seat. She was glad he was thumbing through it and didn't see her biting her lip, trying to focus on the road.

"So, what kind of music do you like?" she asked. "I mean, other than an off-key version of 'If I Loved You.'"

He laughed. "I don't remember, but my favorite band is Providence. No, wait—that's the next town over from the hospital."

She laughed with him.

"Will you play for me?" he asked.

The request surprised her. "I play mostly classical."

"Don't worry," he said with a wry smile. "I can't remember what I like."

A few minutes later she parked the car in the church lot. "I need to get the key from the rectory."

Guy followed her to a small, shingled building that was

attached by a covered passageway to the church. Its windows were open and Ivy could hear the doorbell ringing inside. Then Father John's voice called from behind another building. "In the back!"

Guy, who was wearing jeans, quickly pulled the cuffs of his sweatshirt down to his wrists. They found the priest in the garden, wearing denim overalls, his hands caked with sandy dirt, his high cheekbones shining with sweat and sun. Ivy introduced him to Guy.

Father John held up both hands apologetically and gave a slight bow. "My day off," he explained.

"You're working awfully hard for that," Ivy observed.

He smiled. "A labor of love."

Inside a white picket fence was a large vegetable garden. A trench, partially dug along the outside of the fence, had bags of peat and humus piled next to it.

"I'm putting in roses," he said, gesturing. "Of course, we have the Rugosa—beach roses—here on the Cape. It's very foolish of me to be digging holes in the sand and bringing in black soil to grow *tea* roses." He shrugged and smiled.

Ivy saw Guy relax a little.

"You're here to play," the priest guessed, reaching for the set of keys that hung on his belt. "Would you bring these back as soon as you've opened up?"

Guy went with Ivy as far as the church door, then offered to return the keys. Fifteen minutes later, when he hadn't come back to the church, Ivy sighed—sudden departures seemed to be Guy's favorite way of saying good-bye. Having finished her exercises, she pushed Guy out of her mind and focused on the new music assigned by her teacher. She worked hard, and her tentative fingering became more certain. Ivy never got over the wonder of feeling a song grow under her hands.

An hour later, gathering up her music, she heard the church door open. Guy walked toward her, looking pleased with himself. "I've got a job."

"You do?"

His face gleamed with perspiration and there was a smear of dirt down the front of his sweatshirt. He pointed in the direction of the garden, his hand coated with sandy soil. "I was helping him out—just for something to do. And he asked if I liked that kind of work. He's going to set me up with one of his parishioners who's looking for summer help."

"Great! He didn't care if you had references?"

"I made up a name and cell phone number," Guy replied.

"What?"

"With a little luck, the man won't bother to check."

"It's just that—" Ivy didn't finish her statement. The bruise on Guy's face had faded beneath his tan and was barely noticeable. It was a breezy morning, and it may not have seemed odd to the priest that Guy hadn't removed his sweatshirt or rolled up his sleeves to work.

"You don't trust me," he said. "Will has been filling your head with doubts—"

Ivy felt defensive of Will. "Don't blame him. I'm quite capable of doubting on my own."

Guy's eyes met hers, then he threw back his head and laughed. "You're so honest!" He sat down in a pew, draping his arms across the back of the bench. "Play something for me. I have a strong feeling I'm not a classy guy and will be easy to impress."

"The song you were humming was from a musical. I have a pile of Broadway songs home in Connecticut." She flipped through the books she had brought, looking for something light and melodic. "A guy I loved once liked musicals."

"You don't love him anymore?"

Ivy met Guy's eyes. "No, I still do. I always will."

"He dumped you," Guy guessed.

"He died."

Guy dropped his arms from the back of the church bench. "I'm sorry—I didn't realize. . . . How?" he asked gently.

"He was murdered."

Guy rose to his feet. "Jesus Christ!"

Ivy took a deep breath. "Is that a prayer? You're in the right place."

Guy continued to stare at her, and she made herself busy looking for music. "This'll work—Brahms." She began to play.

Guy circled the piano, still staring at her, his hands in his pockets, then he strolled down the side aisle. He stopped at each stained glass window and seemed to study it. Was he reading the images or peering through them, Ivy wondered; was he seeing the present or catching glimpses of the past? More than ever, her past with Tristan seemed to intrude into her everyday life.

Focus on the present, she told herself, and glanced toward Guy. *Focus on someone who needs your help now*. Maybe the music would relax his mind and allow him to recall bits of what he was repressing. She finished Brahms, and continued with music she knew by heart: the first movement of Beethoven's Piano Sonata, Number 14. By the final measures Guy was standing behind her.

"You're playing from memory," he said as the last note faded.

Ivy nodded.

"I can't remember my own name," he observed, "but you can play an entire song from memory."

Ivy swallowed hard. Better to have the pain in her heart forever than to lose her memory of Tristan—Guy had taught her that much.

"It's a song you love, or maybe one *he* loved," Guy guessed.

Ivy closed the piano and gathered up her pieces of music. "Yes."

"'Moonlight Sonata,'" Guy said. "The first part of Beethoven's Sonata Fourteen."

Ivy's turned to him, surprised.

Guy took a step back. "Whoa! How'd I know that?"

They gazed at each other, mirroring amazement, then Ivy smiled. "And you thought you weren't a classy guy!"

IVY AND GUY STOOD AT THE TOP OF THE STEPS BY Chatham Light, the same place Ivy and Will had stood eight days earlier. In the afternoon sun, the wide stretch of sand, more than a quarter mile deep, burned hot and white. The ocean swept past, curving to the south as far as the eye could see, its color like the blue sea glass that Ivy loved.

They had picked up sandwiches and soda at a café near the church, and Ivy had given Guy the beach towel she had brought along. "Would you like me to come back in an hour? It's a long walk to Nickerson," she added, "and I'll be driving home in that direction."

Guy kept his eyes on the beach, and after a moment asked, "Would you come with me?"

She was careful not to gush *Of course—I was hoping—whatever I can do to help.*

"Sure. I like the beach," she replied, and started down the steps.

Reaching the sand, she stepped aside to let Guy lead the way, not wanting to do anything that might extinguish a spark of memory. She followed him across the beach, removing her shoes as he did when they reached the damp sand, then walking next to him, heading south. Toddlers played at the sea's frothy edge, running back and forth with plastic pails. A father played Frisbee with his kids. A middle-aged woman with wet, spiky hair smiled to herself as she carried her raft from the waves. Beneath a striped umbrella a younger boy played checkers with an older one and let out a shout of victory. Thinking about the way Philip had loved to play the game with Tristan, Ivy turned for another look and saw that Guy had stopped to watch the pair.

"You were frowning," Ivy said when they moved on.

"I thought—for a moment I thought I knew that kid, the little one."

They strolled on in silence and passed a sign that prohibited swimming from that point south.

"The officer who interviewed me said that they found me about fifty yards beyond the no-swimming sign."

They walked that distance and Guy stopped to survey the area. "Not very smart of me," he remarked dryly, "to swim at midnight in an area with dangerous currents."

"Are you sure you were swimming?" she asked.

"The doctors said there was enough seawater in me to drown an army."

"Okay, but it's obvious from your injuries you were in some kind of fight. Maybe you were knocked unconscious at the edge of the ocean and the tide came in. Do you know how to swim?" she asked.

He was standing back from the water as if he didn't like the feel of it washing over his feet.

"Doesn't everybody?" he replied.

"No, not everybody."

He dropped his eyes. "The water . . . it bothers me. I don't want to get in. It scares me," he admitted, climbing the bank to the dryer sand.

"After what happened to you, it should," Ivy replied, following him, laying the beach towel where he dropped his backpack, about twenty feet beyond the tidal line. "It's okay to be afraid, Guy. Anyone who had nearly drowned would be."

He pulled off his sweatshirt and T-shirt. It took Ivy's breath away, the strength and the vulnerability she saw in him. His back and shoulders were broad and muscular, but his skin a pale, grayish green with fading bruises.

"None of this looks familiar," he said, surveying the distant houses spread beyond the dunes.

He sat on the towel close to Ivy. The desire to put her arms around him, to shield him from the confusion and fear that haunted him, was so strong that she had to look away. *Water Angel, help him,* she prayed, then asked, "Do you believe in angels?"

"No. Do you?"

"Yes," she said firmly. Peeking sideways, she saw the corners of Guy's mouth curling upward. Tristan had once worn the same amused expression.

"I believe there are people who *act* like angels," Guy added, "showing up unexpectedly at the moment you need them. Like the little boy who gave me this." He reached in his pocket, pulling out a gold coin stamped with an angel. "He came to my hospital room and started jawing with me like he had known me all his life. There was something about that kid, the way he looked at me—it was as if he could see through me and understood something I didn't."

Ivy took the coin from him. "That kid—he's my brother."

"Your brother." Guy's eyes narrowed, as if he was trying hard to remember something.

Ivy's cell phone went off and they both turned toward her bag. After a minute, the familiar ringtone stopped, then it began all over again.

"Aren't you going to answer it?" Guy asked.

Ivy handed the coin back to him. "Later. I, uh, want to get my feet wet," she said, and headed toward the waves. She felt as if she couldn't fight it anymore than she could fight the sea, this deep connection she felt with Guy. It was a relief to stand in the surf, the ocean rushing against her legs, making her skin cold and tingly. Tristan had taught her to swim, and after Gregory had died, Ivy had taken lessons, becoming an even stronger swimmer. Still, her feet fought the undertow and her arms prickled with the ocean's spray. She was both afraid of and seduced by the sea.

She stood there for a long time, then moved closer to the shore, crouching to look at a sparkling crescent of shells and pebbles. When she glanced up, Guy was standing ten feet away, watching her so closely she became self-conscious. She stood up, and at the same time, he moved toward her, smiling.

"Your hair!" he said

Feeling the wind tossing it this way and that, she reached back and caught her hair, holding it still. "What about it?"

"You should see it. It's . . . wild."

She imagined it looked like kinky gold seaweed blowing in the wind. "Hey, do you see me laughing at yours?" *Not that there is any reason to*, she thought. His streaky blond hair had a curl to it—like hair an Italian sculptor might give a hero.

Guy laughed, then glanced over his shoulder. Her cell was ringing again. They caught a snatch of it before the breeze carried off the sound.

"Same ringtone," he observed. "For some reason, it sounds to me like Will."

"It is."

"I made him nervous yesterday."

When Ivy didn't comment, Guy went on. "I thought about telling him that he had nothing to worry about. . . . Does he have anything to worry about?"

"Like what?"

He smiled. "Well, when I was making the great escape from the hospital, I asked if I should say that I was your boyfriend. You quickly corrected me—*brother*, you said."

Ivy gazed downward and turned over a shell with her toe, as if fascinated by how it might look on the opposite side.

"A girl who quickly informs you that you cannot be her boyfriend is one of two things: very committed to her boyfriend, or feeling guilty because she's not."

Ivy crouched to pick up the shell.

"Which was it?" he asked.

She didn't reply. Rising to her feet, she attempted to distract him from the question by holding out the shell to him. But instead of looking at it, he caught a piece of her hair.

The light tug of his hand, the way he opened his palm and looked down at the lock of her hair, made her heart pound. His gaze was hidden beneath golden lashes. Then he raised his eyes and caught her mass of hair in both hands, lifting it away from her face. His hands slid to the back of her neck with the gentleness of someone cupping a flower. Gazing at her mouth, he bent his head, moving his face slowly closer to hers.

A rush of cold water pushed them apart.

"Sorry, I—it startled me. The water," he said, looking embarrassed.

"Me too." After a moment of uncomfortable silence, she added, "I'm starved. Why don't we have our lunch now?"

He nodded and they returned to the beach towel, where they ate in silence. As Ivy took the last bite of her sandwich, her cell phone went off again. Guy hummed along with the familiar ring, and grinned at Ivy. She dug into her bag.

"I knew you'd give in sooner or later."

"Did you?" she replied. Leaving the phone in the bag, she pulled out a paperback and sunglasses, and began to read.

Guy laughed, then spread his sweatshirt behind her and his T-shirt behind him. In five minutes he was asleep— Ivy knew it by his slow and even breaths.

She reached in her bag for her phone. Three calls and three texts from Will. One call, no message, from Beth. Ivy looked at Will's first text: WHERE R U?

Can't I go anywhere without telling you? she thought, then felt guilty. She clicked on the second message. It was an apology for whatever Will had said in his voicemails. Ivy moved on to the third, deciding not to listen to the voicemails—things between them were strained enough.

R U OK? Will wrote. B SAYS SOMETHING IS WRONG. 1 OF THOSE FEELINGS SHE GETS. MAKING ME CRAZY.

Ivy sighed. She couldn't blame Will for worrying when Beth went on like that, but this time Beth was wrong.

@ BEACH. HOME 4 DINNER, Ivy typed to Will and Beth, then turned off her phone and dropped it in her bag.

Gazing down at Guy, Ivy reached, and with light fingers, touched his hair. She lay down close to him, wanting, for the first time in a year, to live in no other time but the present.

Fourteen

IT WAS NEARLY SIX O'CLOCK WHEN IVY DROPPED GUY off at Nickerson. Arriving at the Seabright's lot, she noticed a bright yellow sports car parked next to Kelsey's Jeep and Dhanya's Audi. Hearing voices in the direction of the cottage, Ivy checked her messages before following the path from the lot to the cottage. Will had written that Dhanya's and Kelsey's new friends were coming over for a cookout: Y DON'T U STOP BY SOMETIME? he had added. His concern had changed to sarcasm, and in a way, that was easier for her to handle.

Emerging from the path, she saw that the barbecue had begun. An old banquet table had been dragged out from Aunt Cindy's shed and covered with a checkered cloth. Extra chairs had been borrowed from the inn's porch. Will was poking at coals in the grill and glanced up at her as she approached. "Nice of you to show," he remarked, and went back to work.

Beth set large bowls of pretzels and chips on the long table and turned back to the cottage as if she didn't see Ivy.

"Hey," Ivy greeted her.

Beth looked over her shoulder, then glanced toward Will, which annoyed Ivy. It was as if all that mattered was how Will felt.

"Hey, girl. Where ya been?" Kelsey sang out. She and a dark-haired guy were setting up a badminton net.

"Around," Ivy replied. "Looks like I got here just in time."

"You did, and now you've got clean-up duty!"

Ivy laughed. For once she was glad to be around a partygirl with a big voice. It sure beat Beth's and Will's icy welcome.

"Cans are in the cooler. Nothing good," Kelsey said with a flick of her head toward the inn. Ivy assumed she meant nothing alcoholic, not around Aunt Cindy.

"Back in a minute," Ivy replied, and went inside.

Dhanya was in the kitchen, whipping together a dip,

her arm jingling with gold, silver, and copper bracelets. A guy relaxed in a kitchen chair, watching her. It had to be Max, Ivy thought, noticing the shirt. It was Hawaiian silk, and its bright aqua and lime green floral stood in contrast to his monochrome coloring: tan skin, faded-brown hair, and when he turned to look at Ivy, light brown—almost amber— eyes. He smiled, his row of perfect white teeth gleaming against his beige coloring.

"Max Moyer," he said, holding out his hand.

"Ivy Lyons," she replied, walking over to him, amused that he had offered to shake hands but remained in his chair, his foot casually propped on his knee. Glancing down, Ivy recognized his brand of boat shoe—Gregory had worn the same ones.

"I've heard lots about you," Max said.

"How much do you think is true?" Ivy asked.

Her quick reply seemed to catch him off guard. She smiled, and after a moment Max matched her smile.

"All of it. Dhanya wouldn't lie to me."

Dhanya glanced over her shoulder, but said nothing.

"Still," Ivy said, "you should only believe the good stuff." She turned to Dhanya. "Hey. What're you making?"

"Cream cheese and dill. Tell me what you think," Dhanya said, dipping a clean spoon in her mix and holding it out to Ivy.

"Mmm. I think I'm sitting wherever you put this bowl."

"Can I taste?" Max dipped a cracker. "Awesome!" he exclaimed, and then dipped his half-eaten cracker into the communal bowl. Dhanya glanced at Ivy, shook her head, and fastidiously scraped out the section where he had just scooped.

Trying not to laugh—at Dhanya or Max—Ivy headed upstairs to change into a clean top and shorts.

When she joined the others outside, Max was standing next to Will, watching him slide burgers onto the grill.

"You're not planning to join a frat?" he said to Will, his light eyes round with surprise. "What are you going to do all day? You'll die of boredom."

"I'll think of something. Studying for instance."

"But how are you going to meet people?" Max persisted. "Facebook's good, but *fraternities*, they're the melting pot of America."

Will laughed. "Never thought of them that way."

Beth sat a few feet away from them, listening. It wasn't unusual for Beth to be silently observant at social events—taking mental notes, happily gathering dialogue and details for her stories. But the "happily" part was missing, Ivy thought, studying her friend's face. It looked more like Beth was cramming for a test.

"Doesn't anyone want to play with us?" Kelsey called from the badminton game.

"You're going at it way too seriously for me," Ivy replied,

carrying a soda over to the swing. Dusty followed her, and she lifted her hands so the cat could jump in her lap.

"And for me," Max said. "With *Bryan*, I play only electronic games."

Kelsey's competitor, who was medium height but powerfully built, pointed to his friend, lifted his elbows, and squawked like a chicken.

Max shrugged it off.

"So let's quit. I'm thirsty anyway," Bryan said to Kelsey, then strode toward the ice chest and foraged through the frozen chips. "No Red Bull?"

"Just Mountain Dew and Coke," Dhanya answered.

Max toasted Dhanya with his can, then said to Bryan, "This is a classy affair."

"Then we should at least have wine," Bryan mumbled, grabbing a Coke. He sat on the swing next to Ivy, which made the cat jump off.

"I like you, too, kitty," Bryan said to Dusty, then turned to Ivy. "And you are?"

Kelsey blew threw her lips. "You know who she is."

"Ivy," Max told his friend.

"Will's one and only," Kelsey added.

"Well, that's very limiting," Bryan responded.

Ivy fought the urge to roll her eyes. "Nice to meet you."

Both his build and his movement indicated that Bryan was a good athlete. He wore a T-shirt with BOSTON UNIVERSITY printed across his massive chest and shorts that bore the college's insignia. His thick dark hair and green eyes were striking. His Irish complexion gave him a ruddier tan than Max's.

"We were telling Bryan and Max about your accident," Kelsey said to Ivy, dragging a lawn chair over to the swing, "how your car was totaled and all."

"I would never have known it, looking at you and Beth now. How are you feeling?" Bryan asked.

"Fine. The same as before."

Max leaned forward. "What kind of car ran you off the road?"

"Probably a Ferrari Four Fifty-eight," Bryan quipped. "That's what Maxie owns. People with Ferraris always drive like they own the road."

"All I could see were the headlights," Ivy explained, "so I have no idea what it was."

"Were the headlights low to the road?" Max asked, spooning the bowl of dip with his half-eaten pretzel.

Ivy glanced toward Beth, then said, "Neither of us was thinking like witnesses to an accident. We didn't notice those kinds of details."

Bryan nodded and laid his hand on her arm. "Must have been a pretty scary scene." Kelsey, facing Ivy and Bryan, put her feet on the swing between them. "I wonder whatever happened to that guy who was in the hospital when you were, Ivy—you know, our friendly local amnesiac."

Out of the corner of her eye, Ivy saw Will stiffen.

"Our friendly local amnesiac?" Max repeated.

"Yeah, some guy they fished out of the ocean in Chatham, the same night as Ivy's and Beth's accident."

"Really?!" Bryan said with surprise. Then he turned to Max: "Do you think he went to your party?"

"No," Kelsey said. "I would have remembered him. He was gorgeous—even beat-up. He has these incredible, seductive eyes. "

It lasted no more than a half second, the flash in Bryan's eyes, but Ivy had seen it. Kelsey had succeeded in pushing the little green button in him—and in Will. But Bryan was better at covering up his jealous moment; Will continued to scowl.

"I don't know about *that*," Dhanya replied. "I thought the guy was kind of scary."

"Amnesia," Bryan said thoughtfully. "Why didn't I think of that? *I don't know, Officer, none of this looks familiar. . . . I have no idea, Mom. . . . Really, babe? I can't remember anything.* What a great excuse!"

Will snickered.

Ivy changed the subject. "Do you play a sport for BU?"

"Hockey."

"Yeah?" Will replied, interested. "They've got a great team."

"How long have you been playing?" Ivy asked.

"I can't even remember the first time I stood on a pair of skates and held a stick. I think I was six months old."

Kelsey laughed. "A child prodigy. He could walk at six months!"

Bryan grinned at her. "No, but I could skate."

"Your dad was into hockey?" Ivy guessed.

"My mom. She was from a hockey family—all brothers. I work for my uncle, who owns the rink in Harwich. Every year I come to the Cape to help him with summer hockey camps. And I work out, keeping in shape for the season."

"Six a.m., he's at the freakin' rink at six a.m. every morning," Max told them, "even if he has to drive there from a party."

"Max exaggerates," Bryan said, turning back to Ivy, flashing a bad-boy smile, "I always leave parties by four thirty, so I can get in an hour of sleep before I hit the ice."

Ivy simply raised an eyebrow and Bryan laughed good-naturedly. "So how about coming around for some lessons? Private lessons," he added, raising an eyebrow back at her. "I'm a good teacher."

Uh-oh, Ivy thought.

"We're out of salsa," Kelsey said. "Your turn to fetch, Ivy."

"Glad to," she replied, vacating her place on the swing, figuring Kelsey would be sitting there when she returned.

Little green buttons everywhere.

Fifteen

ON THE FIRST DAY OF WORK AUNT CINDY HAD MADE
it clear that, at an inn, where your job was to be cheerfully
helpful to guests, arguing or turning a cold shoulder to
another employee was prohibited. "Get over it or fake it,"
she had said.

Tuesday morning, Ivy and Will were assigned to the
breakfast room; they faked it. But when a toddler threw his
jelly toast on the floor, and the two of them bent over at the
same time and knocked heads, Ivy began to giggle.

"I've got it," Will told her, reaching for the goopy toast.

Before Ivy could straighten up, the toddler poured milk over the side of his booster chair. Ivy felt a splash on her head, followed by liquid dribbling down her back. Will stared at her sopping hair and Ivy laughed at his expression. Grabbing a table linen, he started blotting her head, which made them both laugh.

By the time the tables were cleared and the dishes in the dishwasher, most of yesterday's tension had disappeared. "We should leave here about two forty-five," Will told Ivy as they left the inn together. "After we get the bonfire permit, we can check out Race Point, then find a place for dinner in Provincetown."

"Sounds good," Ivy replied.

At the cottage, she picked up her music and headed to church. She was determined to make her practice as regular and focused as it had been in Connecticut. But as Ivy warmed up at the keyboard, her mind continually played back moments from yesterday—Guy standing behind her as she played the sonata, Guy lowering his head close to hers as they stood at the edge of the sea.

At last she got back her concentration and worked hard for more than an hour. When she finished, she played songs she knew by heart—"To Where You Are," then "Moonlight Sonata." Several measures into Beethoven, she stopped. She was thinking about Guy, about the way he had wandered about the church while she played, and how he had known the name of the piece. She was thinking about Guy when playing Tristan's song! She dropped her hands in her lap.

"Why did you stop?"

Ivy's head jerked up. "I didn't hear you come in."

"I know." Guy was sitting on the end of a pew, halfway down the aisle of the small church. "About ten minutes ago you were playing like a crazy woman, like you were performing at Lincoln Center."

Lincoln Center? He knew what the concert hall was—another clue about his life, slight as it might be. "How was work?" she asked.

"You didn't tell me why you stopped," he replied.

Ivy turned all the way around on the piano bench. "I don't tell you everything."

He smiled and let her off the hook. "Work was terrific. It felt good to be doing something physical and thinking about nothing but what I was doing. The guy, Kip McFarland, is in his twenties and has a small landscaping business. The pay's low, but it's a start, and there's a fringe benefit."

"Which is?"

"I get to sleep with the lawnmowers in an old barn. It has one window that isn't covered, a toilet, and an outside shower. It also has a pile of useless stuff I'm supposed to clean out. Want to come see it?"

"A pile of useless stuff? How could I resist?"

A few minutes later, with Guy supplying directions, Ivy drove to Willow Pond, which was off Route 6A, close to the bay side of the cape. A crushed stone drive led them through woods to an old clapboard house with gables and a wraparound porch. With a lot of hard work—and gallons of paint—the house, its weeping trees, and the round pond reflecting them would look like a scene on one of Aunt Cindy's jigsaw puzzles.

"Kip and his wife bought the house last fall and are restoring it," Guy said. "They want to run a B and B some day, but they need money, so he does carpentry and landscaping, while she teaches, and in the summer helps him with the business."

Guy led Ivy past the right side of the house to the barn. The gray wood structure leaned noticeably toward the surrounding woods, like a building seeking shade.

"Home sweet home," he said. "If you tilt your head, it looks straight."

Ivy grinned. "I can't wait to see inside."

Moving from the bright June day into the building's darkness, Ivy couldn't see anything at first, but she could smell.

"I know," Guy said, hearing her sniff. "You get used to it."

"Mulch. And fertilizer. Some . . . very rich fertilizer."

As her eyes grew accustomed to the dim lighting she

saw the mountain of stuff that needed to be cleared out—furniture, books, lamps, lobster pots, and fishing gear that looked old enough to have been used by the pilgrims.

"Is there a light in here?"

He pointed. "Over the rider mower. Everything on that side is equipment for the landscaping business." He picked up an old lantern. "Kip's wife is lending me this." When he lit it, the lantern's heavy, ringed glass glowed warmly.

"Oh, I like it!"

"I thought you might. Hey, here comes my new roommate, Fleabag."

A skinny black-and-white cat had slipped through the open door and was sauntering toward them.

"You're kidding, right?"

"About the fleas or us being roomies?"

"Both."

Guy set down the lantern. "Well, I was here for twenty minutes when Kip was showing me the place, and Fleabag scratched himself for about ten of those minutes, then flopped down on my backpack."

"I'll get him some flea medicine."

"You'll be more successful getting it for me. Kip said it took forever to trap him and get him to a vet. He's too feral to adopt, but he enjoys showing up now and then and hanging out. You can see why we're meant for each other," Guy added dryly.

"Yes." Ivy surveyed the mess around them. "So where exactly are you going to sleep? You could try that rafter, if you don't mind hanging upside down by your feet."

"I don't mind, but I'm guessing it's already taken by the bats. Thanks to you, however, I have my bedroll. I'll just have to clear a space."

"Let's get started," she said.

"Now?"

"With two of us, it will be easier to move the big things," Ivy told him. She eyed the cat. "And I don't think your roomy is going to lift a paw."

"He will when we disturb a nest of mice."

"Till then," Ivy replied, picking up a chair with a missing leg and heading toward the door. She carried it out to the portable Dumpster that she had seen between the house and barn.

Guy followed with a bent floor lamp and old radio. "If we can get the two sofas out of there," he said, "we'll have some elbow room to work."

A short sofa with exposed springs was fairly easy to move, but the other one, a sleeper that kept unfolding, was twice as heavy. Ivy and Guy tugged and pulled and dragged.

"How are you doing?" Guy asked when they were almost to the door.

Sweat dripped in her eyes and made tiny rivulets

between her ears and cheeks. "Okay. Hey! Look how clean your floor is where we've scraped it."

"That's where my bedroll will go," he said. "Why don't we leave this here for now? I'll ask Kip about using his trailer. If we drag the sofa across the lawn, we're going to take the grass with us, roots and all."

"Agreed."

They found brooms among Kip's lawn equipment and swept the concrete floor, beginning to make a space for Guy, then set to work on the pile of stuff. It was a kind of treasure hunt, and they began calling out "Loot!" when one of them found something of interest—a lamp base shaped like a rearing horse, magazines from the sixties, a turntable with a scratched record still on it—"Chad and Jeremy," Ivy read from the label, then shrugged and carried it outside.

They settled into a comfortable rhythm, examining, sharing, walking back and forth to the Dumpster. At one point Ivy saw Guy walk into the shed with an armful of *National Geographic*s. "Excuse me, I just put those out," she said.

"I know, but they looked interesting."

He placed them next to his bedroll, with the magazines from the sixties. After rolling out a rusty push mower, he returned with a stack of old science books. This time Ivy didn't comment; after all, it was his place.

Between the two of them, they carried out a heavy sink.

"Look at this!" he said, holding up several sports books filled with pictures and large print, apparently written for children. He tucked them under his arm and carried them back to the shed.

When, two hours and many books and magazines later, he added to his stacks the cookbooks that Ivy had just carried to the Dumpster, she could keep silent no longer. "Did you happen to notice you don't have a kitchen?"

"I might someday."

Ivy laughed.

"Time for a break. Let's sit in the living room," he said, gesturing to the bedroll. "Something to drink?" He opened his backpack and drew out two bottles of water.

Ivy took a long drink, then wiped her sweaty face on her sleeve.

"Nice shade of dirt you're wearing," he remarked.

She touched her cheek.

"Other side," he said, then reached and softly wiped that cheek.

For a moment, Ivy couldn't breathe, couldn't speak. She was under a spell from the touch of his fingers. Then something brushed past them—Fleabag. Ivy quickly turned away from Guy, acting as if her attention had been caught by the cat.

"Now you show up," Guy grumbled to Fleabag, then rested against his backpack. "It's shaping up. I like it," he said, surveying the piles of books and magazines encircling them. "It's homey."

Homey, thought Ivy. That was how she would describe the house where Tristan had lived with his parents. She remembered the first time she saw it, when Tristan adopted her cat, Ella. Their living room was buried under books and magazines.

"You're smiling," Guy said.

She shifted back to the present. "It's comfortable, but not my dream home."

"What is your dream home?" he asked curiously.

"A small house on the water. Living room, kitchen, and bedroom, a porch facing east, another facing west, and two fireplaces. How about yours?"

"I'd live inland, in a fancy tree house."

Ivy laughed.

"It would have several levels—and be built between two trees," Guy continued.

"I know a place like that."

"It would have a rope ladder, of course. And a swing."

Ivy loved the swing that hung under Philip's tree house, which was near the edge of her family's property. High on the ridge above the river and train tracks, the view was spectacular.

"And it would be high on a ridge, so I could see over the countryside."

Ivy looked at Guy with surprise.

"What is it?" he asked.

"That's exactly like my brother's." Her mind slipped back to the day that Philip had almost fallen from the tree house's walkway. Gregory had never admitted to loosening the board, and Ivy, who had lost her faith in angels, had not seen the golden shimmer that Philip had. But she believed now, as Philip did, that Tristan was there for him.

Was Tristan here still?

I'll always be with you, Ivy. She heard the words now as clearly as she had the night of the accident, when Tristan kissed her. Ivy knew the old saying—the eyes were the windows of the soul—and sometimes when she looked in Guy's eyes, it was as if Tristan . . .

No, she was imagining it.

"Ivy, you're trembling."

He touched her hands lightly and she tried to make them still in her lap.

"Tell me," he said.

Ivy shook her head no. Guy was confused enough about his identity, without her telling him that he made her feel as if Tristan was present.

"Sometimes you look so sad," Guy said. "I don't know how to help you."

Ivy touched his face gently. "I know how you feel—sometimes you look so lost."

Sixteen

IT WAS A SERIES OF COINCIDENCES, IVY TOLD HER-
self as she turned onto Cockle Shell Road. She had left Guy
in his "homey" place with a new ice chest and leftovers
from the early dinner they had purchased in town. Guy
had asked her to stay longer, but she needed time to think.
She couldn't keep her mind from running through the odd
moments that linked Guy with Tristan. If she dared to tell
Will and Beth what she was starting to believe, she knew
what they would say: She was imagining it—it was just the
anniversary.

The anniversary! Oh, no! She had completely forgotten about going with Will to get the fire permit. When she and Guy had driven to the takeout place, she hadn't bothered to check her cell phone and had totally forgotten about dinner in Provincetown.

Will's car was gone from the Seabright's lot. Ivy walked slowly down the path to the cottage. She was thinking about how she would explain when she heard his Toyota pull in. She stopped and waited nervously. When Will approached the house, he walked fast, his head down.

"Will," she said softly.

He looked up sharply and she could read in his face all the emotions he was feeling: relief, disbelief, and anger.

"Will, I'm so sorry!" She lifted her hand to reach toward him, then quickly dropped it to her side; something—she didn't know what—stopped her from touching him. "I'm so sorry," she repeated.

A long silence followed.

"That's it?" he asked.

"I've let you down."

He swore under his breath.

"I'm really sorry, Will. I just . . . forgot."

"Do you have amnesia too?" he replied sarcastically. "Is it contagious?" His eyes bored through her. "That's where you've been, isn't it? With *him*, with Guy."

"Yes."

"I can't believe it! Why do girls do stuff like this—run after guys who seem mysterious and exciting, but have nothing to offer."

"I'm not running after—"

He cut her off. "I love you, Ivy, but this is killing me."

She swallowed hard.

"Why are you doing this to me?" he shouted at her.

"I don't know!" she shouted back.

She saw him struggle to control his anger; in some ways, she wished he'd keep shouting.

"You're acting like you did after Tristan's death, when Gregory seduced you—"

"What?!"

"And you kept standing up for him," Will continued, "when you kept trusting Gregory even though there were a million signs that you shouldn't."

"Like you weren't Gregory's friend, too?" Ivy challenged him.

"I recognized him for what he was and stayed friends long enough to help you and Tristan." Will sucked in his breath. "*Tristan*. It always comes back to him, doesn't it? God, what an idiot I am!"

Ivy lowered her head.

"The night you were in the accident, when I got to the hospital, the paramedic asked me if I was Tristan."

Ivy winced.

"He said you had been calling for him in the ambulance."

Ivy turned away.

"Then the doctor, elated with your progress, came to me and said, '*I've got good news for you, Tristan.*'"

Ivy shut her eyes with the pain. Will had kept this to himself, even though it must have hurt him deeply.

"Here's what I think," Will said, his voice husky with emotion. "I don't think you're really falling for Guy. I think you feel bad for him and find him a nice distraction."

Ivy turned back toward Will.

He went on quickly. "With Guy, you can feel for somebody, help somebody, and still be in love with Tristan."

"Will, I am so sorry—"

"This fling with Guy, it helps you to separate from me," Will continued. "The best thing I can do for you and for me is make the final break that you clearly want so much." His voice grew angrier. "It would have been a lot easier on both of us, Ivy, if you'd had the guts to tell me when you knew it was over!"

"But I didn't know—"

He slammed his fist into his palm. "Give me a break!"

"I knew something was wrong," Ivy explained. "I was trying to think things through."

He nodded. "And why end it when it may turn out that you need me after all?"

"No! That's unfair! I wouldn't have used you like that."

"Next time you're thinking things through, try thinking about how it is for someone other than yourself." He turned on his heel and headed back to the parking lot.

"Where are you going, Will?"

"I don't know. I don't care, as long as it's somewhere away from you."

THE TEARS THAT HAD BEEN FILLING IVY'S EYES DURING the argument did not fall until five minutes after Will had driven away. Ivy walked back to the lot and stood motion-less by her car, watching the road as if Will might come back. "It's over. Over," she repeated to herself with disbelief. She noticed an envelope on her car's front seat. Opening it, she found the permit for the bonfire. She climbed inside her car, closed the door, and cried.

Ivy drove for an hour and a half—Route 6 first, needing to drive fast, and when she had stopped crying, the wind-ing, dual-lane 6A. She was tempted to call her mother—but her mother loved Will. Philip loved Will. Beth loved Will. So did she, but maybe not enough.

By the time she returned to the inn, it was nearly dark. Will's car was back; Kelsey's was gone and no one was in the cottage. Ivy sat in the living room, trying to work on the puzzle, riffling through the box, pulling out one piece, then another, then putting them back. Restless, she walked out-side, glanced at the swing, then strode over to the inn's back steps, where she felt less likely to be cornered by whoever came home first. If Will hadn't told the others about their break up, she would have to share the news before work tomorrow.

Behind her, the kitchen door opened, spreading the room's yellow light on a swath of grass.

"Don't get up," Aunt Cindy said, then came out and sat on the steps next to Ivy. "How are you doing?"

"Okay."

"Pretty tough, huh?"

Ivy nodded. "Yeah. Who told you?"

"Beth. Listen, Ivy, I can make sure that you and Will aren't on the same work team for a week or so, but you'll still be living and working in close quarters. I can't have you quarreling in front of guests, and I can't have the others taking sides."

Ivy nodded.

"If you feel like you can't deal with the situation, you've got to let me know."

"Okay."

Aunt Cindy rested her hand lightly on Ivy's back. "I know it seems as if the pain is so bad that it will never get better. But it will, Ivy. It really will," she said, then went inside.

Ivy rose and walked slowly across the garden. After all the grime and sweat of the day, she'd feel better if she took a shower before facing the others. Then she saw Beth coming around the corner of the renovated barn—from Will's room—Ivy guessed. Ivy took a deep breath and waited.

"How's Will?"

"How are *you*?" Beth asked, as she approached Ivy.

The gentleness in her friend's voice released another, unexpected flood of tears.

"Come on. Let's talk," Beth said, giving Ivy a light push toward the swing.

Beth remained quiet while Ivy cried.

"I feel so bad about hurting him," Ivy said, wiping her eyes.

"I feel bad for both of you," Beth replied, then added softly, "It's hard for Will—and for me—to understand. I mean, after all you've been through together, how can you not love him?"

"I do love him," Ivy insisted. "But maybe not the way he wants to be loved."

Beth leaned forward, looking into Ivy's eyes. "The way *anyone* wants to be loved!"

"Yes, yes, you're right," Ivy admitted. "But, Beth, you can't always choose how you love a person. Love isn't logical or fair. It just happens."

In the faint starlight, Ivy saw the silver trace of a tear running down Beth's face.

"Did you tell him that I saw Tristan the night of the

accident?" Ivy asked.

"That you *thought* you saw Tristan—no. No, he's already convinced he's competing with a dead guy. I'm not going to make it any harder for him. Ivy, did you really forget your date tonight?"

Ivy nodded. "I was with Guy, helping him."

"Guy!"

"Yes, cleaning out a barn, so he'd have a decent place to live, and—"

"Ivy, you have to be careful," Beth warned. "You have no idea who Guy is."

"What I know about him is more important than the name he's forgotten. There's a special connection between Guy and me, something I've felt only once before—with Tristan." Ivy ignored the disapproval that lined her friend's face. "Beth, Guy was telling me about his dream house, and it was exactly like Philip's tree house. Guy couldn't remember what music he liked, but suddenly recognized 'Moonlight Sonata,' Tristan's song. And without even knowing what melody it was, he hummed a song from *Carousel*. Don't you remember—Tristan tried to communicate with me by playing on my piano notes from *Carousel*."

Beth shook her head with disbelief, but Ivy continued. "I think Tristan has come back to me."

"Oh, Ivy, no! That couldn't be."

"Why not?" Ivy asked, grasping the edge of the swing. "He spoke through Will and you last year. Why couldn't he now be speaking through Guy, giving me these signs that he is still with me? The night of the accident, Tristan promised—"

"Does Guy claim to hear another person's voice?" Beth asked.

"No, but—"

Beth leaned forward, placing a hand on Ivy's wrist. "When Tristan was here as an angel, we heard him. When he slipped into our minds, we knew who he was. And we never forgot our own identities."

Ivy pulled away from her friend. They sat for a moment in silence, Ivy fighting her anger with Beth for not believing as she did. When Ivy looked back, Beth was pulling on her amethyst necklace. Her lips moved silently, then she said aloud, "Something evil is walking among us."

"What?"

"Ever since the séance I have felt a presence," Beth said, her voice shaking. "It's him. It's Gregory. I haven't felt this way since he was alive."

Ivy stared at her friend, trying to understand what she was saying. "Beth, I know you were spooked by the séance. We all were. But why would you think that Gregory is haunting us? Has something else happened to scare you?"

Her friend didn't reply.

"Tell me," Ivy said.

"A dream." Beth rubbed one hand with the other, digging her fist into her palm. "I've had it twice."

"Tell me," Ivy insisted.

"We're in the cottage, you, me, Dhanya, Kelsey. It's Aunt Cindy's cottage, but it has lots of windows, windows everywhere. Someone is circling the house, shooting at the windows. The bullets pierce the glass but don't go all the way through. We're running from room to room, and the shooter runs around the outside of the cottage, targeting the windows of whichever room we're in. He keeps circling, but you tell us everything's all right. We're safe, you say, the shooter can't break through the windows. Then he quietly opens the door and walks in."

Ivy sat back in the swing, rubbing her arms, her skin prickling.

"Don't you get it?" Beth said, sounding suddenly angry. "You were careless and let the shooter in, just like you let in Guy!"

"Beth, not every dream you have is clairvoyant. Sometimes you dream about things that people tell you. Will doesn't like Guy. He's planted these fears in you."

Beth's eyes flashed. "It makes no difference what Will says. I see what I see!"

"So do I," Ivy replied, then rose from the swing.

"Ivy!"

She turned back reluctantly.

Beth's hand clutched her amethyst. "If it's Gregory, you will need all the power of heaven to protect you."

Seventeen

"YOU KNOW, I THOUGHT YOU WERE, LIKE, MISS Perfect," Kelsey said to Ivy the next evening. "And when you were hanging with Will, you were, like, Mr. and Mrs. Perfect. Couple of the year."

"Sorry to disappoint you."

"So what exactly did he say to you?" Kelsey asked. They were standing outside the cottage, Kelsey bouncing a badminton birdie up and down on a racket. *Plunk, plunk, plunk.*

"The kind of thing people usually say when they're breaking up," Ivy replied.

"Snide comments and sweeping accusations," Kelsey guessed. "I've done it myself a few times."

"Then I don't need to fill you in."

"He'll get over it," Kelsey said, and flicked her head toward the barn. "He has plenty of sympathy."

Beth had canceled her date with Chase, and Dhanya had decided that she really missed watching TV. Ivy pictured Will on his daybed, with Beth and Dhanya on either side of him, holding him up by the elbows like supportive angels.

"Want to play?" Kelsey asked, extending a badminton racket toward Ivy.

"Okay."

They took warm-up swings, batting the birdie back and forth across the net.

"So, are you dating that gorgeous mystery guy?" Kelsey asked.

"Dating? No."

"Beth told us that's where you were when you forgot about your date with Will."

Ivy caught up with the sinking birdie and flicked it off the rim of her racket. "I was helping Guy clear out a place to live."

"Beth doesn't trust him."

Ivy didn't respond

"Why doesn't she?" Kelsey asked.

"I don't know," Ivy said, and dove for the birdie.

Kelsey appeared to change her strategy, placing her shots in easy reach of Ivy, perhaps thinking that would encourage her to talk more.

"What do you think of Chase?"

"Don't really know him," Ivy replied, reluctant to share her opinion with someone likely to pass it on.

Kelsey rolled her eyes. "Well, five minutes gave me enough time. He's creepy."

"Creepy?" Ivy repeated with an easy swing.

"He's a control freak," Kelsey said. "There's nothing I hate more than a guy who tries to control a girl."

Ivy doubted that any guy had been successful at controlling Kelsey.

"Beth told us about Tristan."

Ivy returned the serve without comment.

"I had no idea! I've never known anyone whose boyfriend was murdered!"

Ivy swatted the birdie hard.

"I wish I could have met Tristan and Gregory," Kelsey continued. "Last summer must have been awesome!"

Ivy stood flat-footed—didn't even swing. What did Kelsey think last summer was, a reality survival show? "Keep your eye on the birdie," Kelsey advised. "Beth said that Will was totally there for you when Tristan died."

"He was. No one could have been kinder."

"But kindness isn't passion," Kelsey replied. "And we like passion."

Ivy returned the serve with a passionate stroke. "Kelsey, don't assume anything about my and Will's relationship."

"I wouldn't have to assume if you filled me in."

In spite of herself, Ivy laughed.

"Beth said you're having a memorial bonfire for Tristan at Race Point. Can Dhanya and I come?"

"I-I'm not sure it's still on."

"It is," Kelsey informed her. "That's another thing I don't like: guys who act loyal and thoughtful, no matter what you do. I mean, what are they trying to prove?"

Ivy dropped the head of her racket. "I've had enough."

"But we haven't started to keep score," Kelsey protested.

Ivy nodded. "A perfect time for me to quit."

Fifteen minutes later, Ivy slipped out the back door of the cottage and drove to the beach on Pleasant Bay where she, Will, and Philip had spent an afternoon a week ago. Sitting on the beach in the deepening twilight, not far from the cluster of trees that Will had sketched, she sifted through memories, trying to understand why it had taken her so long to realize she couldn't give Will her heart.

Rising to her feet, she followed the same route she and Philip had taken around a sandy point to a cove. With no moon, the calm water was bathed in starlight. Ivy remembered the cathedral of stars where Tristan had kissed her. She whispered his name and could almost hear him answer, "My love." Almost. The voice she heard in her head was a memory—she knew that. What she had heard *then* was actually happening. The difference between now and then made the moment after the accident all the more real to her. To Ivy, the embrace was more real than the most tangible and ordinary moments of her life.

But what if it had been Tristan, and Lacey was right about the consequences? *"Serious fallout"*—what did that mean? And what evil presence did Beth sense? Could Gregory return?

"Lacey. Lacey Lovett. I need to talk to you," Ivy called.

She sat by the water's edge, watching, waiting. Minutes ticked by. Across the bay, the yellow edge of the moon peeked over a narrow strip of beach.

"You have the *lousiest* timing!"

Seeing the purple shimmer, Ivy stood up. "Hey, Lacey."

"So what is it this time—another beatific vision? Ivy dancing with the stars?"

Ivy watched the angel twirl, her purple mist dancing in front of the low moon, then said, "Beth is having dreams."

"Beth—the radio?" "Radio" was Lacey's term for a person who was open to "the other side," a natural medium.

"Yes," Ivy said, and recounted the dream.

"When was the first time she had it?"

181

"I'm not sure. Two Sundays ago, when we had a séance—"

"A séance!" Lacey exclaimed. "The radio should know better!"

Ivy described the event, including the strange way the planchette had moved in counterclockwise circles, and how it had seemed impossible for them to slow it down.

"And this happened before your accident?"

Ivy thought back to it. "A few days before."

"*Un*believable. Unbelievable! Do you have a brain? Does the radio have even a shred of common sense, opening up a portal like that to the other side? Are you so narcissistic that you think that only *good* angels hang around you?"

"I—no—I never thought about—meaning we could have let in—"

"*Invited,*" Lacey corrected. "Flagged down, hailed a taxi for—"

"Something evil."

"Something evil," Lacey confirmed.

Ivy crouched and traced a counterclockwise circle in the sand, then another, and another. A hand with purple-painted nails caught her arm. "Stop that!"

"Is it possible for Gregory to come back as a demon?" Ivy asked.

"Obviously, you missed a lot of Sunday school. Anything is possible with Number One Director."

Ivy rose and walked along the cove's waterline. "But why would Gregory return?" she mused to herself.

"Revenge, murder, mayhem . . . ," Lacey suggested.

It was what Beth had been thinking: *If it's Gregory, you will need all the power of heaven to protect you.*

"Revenge against me," Ivy said. "But how would he do that?"

Lacey responded with a loud, theatrical sigh. "Think it through, chick. I'm sure you're not as naïve as you seem. How did Tristan come back?"

"He worked through people's minds. He matched thoughts with us and slipped inside. We could hear him like a voice in our heads—Beth, Will, Philip, and finally, me."

"Later, Eric and Gregory, although I advised him against entering their twisted minds."

Ivy felt as if an icy hand had touched her own. "Gregory could get inside people?"

"Ladies and gentlemen," Lacey said to her imaginary audience, "the chick is catching on."

"He could get into someone's mind and talk?"

"Persuade," Lacey said quietly. "Tempt."

Ivy shivered.

"As you may remember," Lacey added, "Gregory could torture and tempt even when he was alive."

"Could he force someone to do something?"

"Who needs force, when people are so gullible, so

easy to trick and convince? Not mentioning any names, of course."

"How can we fight him?'

"*We?*" Lacey's purple mist began to move away from Ivy. "In my movie days, I did some horror flicks, but I'm not starring in this one. You're on your own."

"How do *my friends* and I fight him?"

"I'm sure you can come up with something. Or maybe the radio can. I have one piece of advice: Be careful who you trust."

Ivy bit her lip.

"Look, chick, I'm sorry about this mess you're in, but I've got my hands full right now. I think I've found my one true gig, and I'm short on time. I've got to cut out these cameo appearances." The angel's violet shimmer was fading. "Say hello to Philip."

Lacey had almost disappeared when Ivy said, "But what if Tristan has come back to protect me from Gregory?"

Her words had the desired effect: "What?!" exclaimed Lacey.

"I've seen the signs. Tristan is with me, as he promised he would be."

Ivy felt a strong hand anchoring her at the bay's edge. "That's a ridiculous idea! If Tristan was here I would see him."

Lacey had a point. Why wasn't she aware of him? Was Tristan hiding inside Guy? Hiding from whom?

"Ivy, if Tristan did give you the kiss of life," Lacey said, "he's in deep trouble. Don't try to contact him. Don't tempt him further. You've already gotten him killed. Don't damn him forever."

Eighteen

LACEY HAD ALWAYS BEEN MELODRAMATIC, IVY TOLD herself, as she sat alone in the cottage Thursday evening.

Beth, Dhanya, and Will had left for a seven-thirty movie. Spurned by Dhanya, Max had roared off with Kelsey and Bryan to a party in Harwich. As soon as they were gone, Ivy took out her phone, playing a message she'd received an hour before, wanting to hear Guy's voice again: "It's me. Kip got me a cell. Want to come over tonight?"

Pushing aside the warnings of Lacey and Beth, Ivy drove to Willow Pond. When she arrived, she saw a pickup parked in front of the house. A dark-haired woman in her late twenties stood next to it, holding open the door for a golden Lab, which lumbered into the passenger seat. The woman called hello to Ivy and introduced herself as Julie, Kip's wife.

"I hope you didn't have special plans tonight," Julie said. "Guy is on the back porch sound asleep. He and Kip started hacking away at tree stumps at six a.m."

Ivy smiled. "Just hanging out."

Ivy walked around the house and found Guy asleep on the porch that faced the pond, lying on a canvas drop cloth, his shirt off, his body turned so that he was on his side, his head resting on his arm. In the evening light, his tanned skin and fair hair looked golden, reminding Ivy of a painting she had seen once of a sleeping angel. Then she remembered the subject of the painting: a fallen angel, after his battle with heaven. She turned and walked toward the pond.

Fleabag was snoozing in the long grass. Ivy sat on the bank not far from the cat, gazing out at the water, enjoying the pond's reflection of the fiery sky and dark green trees. The evening was the first really warm one they'd had on the cape, balmy and sweet-scented, the way summer nights were inland. She waded into the pond. After the brine of the ocean, the freshwater felt soothing to her skin. Her shorts and halter top were as light as a bathing suit. She swam and swam, loving the solitude and peace of the place. When she was tired, she flipped on her back to float.

It's such a great feeling, Ivy. Do you know what it's like to float on a lake, a circle of trees around you, a big blue bowl of sky above you?

Tristan, she called to him silently. *I do know—I know now, Tristan.*

"Hey, are you asleep out there?" Guy shouted to her.

Ivy raised her head, then pulled her feet under her and stood up. "Asleep!" she hollered back. "You're the one who was snoring."

"No way!" He looked around, then pointed. "I think you must have heard Fleabag."

"Cats can't purr *that* loud," she teased, and waded toward shore.

When she was a few feet from Guy, he said, "You looked so happy out there."

"I was. It's such a great feeling, floating on a pond, a circle of trees around you, the sun sparkling at the tips of your fingers and toes."

Perhaps it was a reflection off the water. For a moment Guy's eyes seemed brilliant, the color of Tristan's "big blue bowl of sky."

"Come on in," Ivy coaxed.

Guy looked down at the water that lapped his ankles and swallowed hard. "I don't think I know how to swim."

Ivy tried to hide her disappointment. If Tristan was in Guy, Guy wouldn't fear water as calm as a swimming pool's.

Live in the present moment, Ivy told herself. *Help him, as Tristan helped you.*

Tristan had eased her beyond her fear by suggesting they take "a walk" in the school swimming pool. She reached for Guy's hand. "Come on. Let's go for a walk in the pond."

After a moment of hesitation, Guy took her hand. They walked slowly and quietly together, moving through the liquid gold of the pond. When the water was waist-deep on Guy, Ivy stopped, and ran her fingers across the water's still surface, sending out plum-colored ripples.

She faced Guy, then scooped up water, pouring handfuls over his shoulders and chest. Reaching higher, she bathed his cheeks and forehead, remembering how Tristan had done that for her. "You okay?"

Guy nodded, then smiled sheepishly.

"We won't walk any farther. Can you crouch?" she asked. Bending her legs, she lowered herself until the water reached her chin. Guy did the same, moving slowly and steadily, but when the water touched his neck, he instinctively pulled up.

"Easy does it." She reached for his other hand, holding them both securely in hers.

He lowered himself again, until their faces were inches apart.

"Next time I'll bring a float and give you a real lesson.

Today, we'll just splash around so you can get used to it. Can you put your face in the water?"

He tried, then jerked his head back, straightening up quickly. "This is humiliating. I-I couldn't breathe. My throat closed up and—"

"Symptoms of panic," Ivy said calmly, "which is a rational response after what you've been through. Here." She laid her hands palms up on the surface of the water. "Hold your breath and rest your face in my hands for a moment,"

"I feel stupid."

"No one's watching."

Guy grimaced but did as she said, laying his face in her wet hands. He did it repeatedly, Ivy lowering her hands a bit each time until his face was immersed.

"Okay," Guy said. "I've got that down. This time I'll do it without you. . . . You don't think I'm acting too macho, do you?" he added, laughing at himself.

She grinned back at him. "When your face is in the water, blow out through your nose."

He did the drill several times, then said, "I bet you've never had a student progress this fast. What's next?"

"Going all the way under." Ivy saw the hesitation and the goose bumps on his arms. "But let's just hang out and do that next time."

"I'll do it now," he insisted.

"You have nothing to prove, Guy."

"I'm going all the way under," he said.

"When you're ready—"

"I can handle this!" he told her, and Ivy took a step back. His voice lightened. "Count for me, okay? See how long I can stay under." He quickly dropped below the pond's surface.

Ivy counted aloud, "One thousand one, one thousand two," then saw his back convulse and yanked him upward with all her strength. He had swallowed water and was choking—panicking again.

"You're okay, you're okay," she told him.

He leaned over, holding his stomach. He couldn't stop shaking.

"You're okay, Guy."

He turned away from her, as if ashamed. She put her arms around him from behind and wouldn't let go until he stopped trembling.

"It's . . . the darkness," he said. "Being in the darkness."

"I should have thought about that," she replied. "When Tristan taught me to swim, we were in a clear, well-lit pool."

Guy turned toward her. "Tristan, the guy who died— taught you to swim?"

"Yes. He loved water."

"And you were afraid of it," Guy said.

"Terrified."

Guy reached for Ivy, pulling her to him, holding her

roughly, awkwardly in his arms. She could feel his heart pounding against her. He buried his face in her hair.

"I will never forget you, Ivy," he whispered. "If ever I forget you, there will be nothing but darkness left for me."

BETH AND DHANYA ARRIVED HOME THAT NIGHT before Ivy. She found Dhanya reading, curled in a living room chair, and Beth on the sofa, hunched over the puzzle.

"Hi," Ivy said. "How was the movie?"

"Good," Dhanya replied.

Beth didn't respond, and both girls, looking up, eyed Ivy's damp clothes and hair, not missing a detail.

"You were with him, weren't you," Beth said, making it sound like an accusation rather than a question.

"I was with Guy. Please use his name."

"But that's not his name," Beth pointed out.

"It's his name for now!" Ivy replied, and continued on to the kitchen, where she grabbed a handful of cookies and headed upstairs.

That night, Ivy tossed and turned. Well after the others were asleep, she kicked away her sheets and sat up. Her alarm clock read 2:43 a.m.

She and Beth had tied up the curtain on the window between their beds, but there wasn't a breeze on this unusually warm night. The moon, nearly full, made a bright patch across Beth's bed. Her sheets were on the floor, her face bathed in perspiration, but she slept soundly.

There is nothing harder than being around others and feeling isolated, Ivy thought. She dropped her feet over the side of the bed, debating whether to grab a beach towel and sit outside.

Cht! Cht!

Ivy's head jerked to the left. Something had struck the window—the glass above the screen.

She held still, staring at the window glass. Then, remembering Beth's dream, Ivy turned to her. Beth's eyes moved beneath her lids and her breath was quick—she was dreaming now.

Ivy moved closer to the window. She saw no one among the trees at their end of the house, but the bright moon threw sharp shadows; it would be easy for a person to hide there.

The cottage doors were rarely locked. Feeling slightly uneasy, Ivy pulled on her shorts and headed for the stairway.

Cht! Cht!

She spun around. At the same time Beth sat up. "Ivy?"

"Yes."

"Ivy?" Beth cried out again, sounding frightened.

Ivy hurried back to her. "I'm here."

"It's him. He's shooting at the window!"

Ivy laid a hand on Beth's shoulder, "No, no, it's not." She

sat on the bed. "It was probably something from the trees, seeds or whatever."

"It's him!" Beth insisted, then saw that Ivy was wearing her shorts and shoes. "Don't go outside!"

"Everything's okay. I was just going downstairs to check things."

"Don't! It's him!" Beth's eyes were wide with fear.

Ivy put her arm around her friend. "You've been dreaming, Beth."

"Are the doors locked?"

"I'm going to check them now," Ivy replied, standing up.

"No, Ivy! He'll do anything to get you!"

"Beth, listen to me. You're getting this mixed up with your dream."

Cht! Cht!

They both turned to the window.

"What's that?" Dhanya asked, sitting up in bed. She climbed out and tiptoed across the room to them.

"Don't go near the window," Beth told her. "He'll see you."

"Who will?" Dhanya asked.

"Dhan-ya!" a male voice called.

"Max!" Dhanya and Ivy said at the same time.

"Did you hear? It's just Max," Ivy told Beth, feeling both relieved and annoyed.

Dhanya frowned. "Why is he here? I don't want to talk to him."

"Dhan-ya!"

Ivy went to the window, shoved up the screen, and leaned out. "Go home, Max."

He emerged from the shadows. "Ivy! How are ya?" He sounded pleased to see her—and drunk.

"It's late. Go home."

"I wanna talk to Dhanya," he said.

"She doesn't want to talk to you. Not in the middle of the night."

"Dhan-ya!"

"Shhh!" Ivy pulled back inside the window. "He's going to wake the guests," she told Dhanya.

"Tell that coyote to stop yelping," Kelsey called from her bed. "I need my beauty sleep!"

"I won't speak to him," Dhanya said to Ivy. "I haven't yet decided if I like him." She started back to bed.

"I'm sorry," Ivy said, "but if Max wakes the guests or Aunt Cindy, we're all in trouble. You're coming outside with me. You're talking to him and sending him off."

"You go, girl!" Kelsey cried, then flopped back on her bed.

Beth shook her head, holding her pillow to her chest, as if it were protection.

Dhanya reluctantly put on a robe and shoes, then followed Ivy downstairs.

When Max saw them marching toward him, he stood up, and just as quickly, sank back against a tree. Ivy sighed.

The last thing she wanted to do was drive to Morris Island in the middle of the night, but she couldn't let him drive himself if he wasn't sober.

"Dhanya! You're breakin' my heart!"

Dhanya rolled her eyes.

"How'd you get here?" Ivy asked him.

He pointed unsteadily toward the inn's lot. "Bryne."

Ivy struggled to understand. "Bryan? He's here? Where's your keys?"

"Bryne," Max said again.

Ivy turned to Dhanya. "Talk to him and keep your voices low. I'll check the lot."

The yellow Ferrari sat in the middle of the lot, Bryan in its driver's seat, plugged into his iPod. His eyes were shut.

Ivy called his name several times, then shook him lightly. Startled out of his sleep, he swung his whole body toward her, fist raised.

"Hey! Hey, it's me."

"Ivy!" he said, surprised, and dropped his arm.

"Have you been drinking?"

He pulled out his cell phone to check the time. "Not for two hours." He sounded clearheaded.

"Would you mind getting out of the car?" she asked.

He laughed. "Want me to walk a line, officer?"

"Yup."

He complied, grinning.

"Listen," Ivy said, "your buddy isn't scoring any points with Dhanya. Take Max home . . . quietly."

Bryan nodded. "Understood. I apologize."

He retrieved Max, who, after simply talking with Dhanya, seemed to be a happier camper.

Ivy and Dhanya wearily entered the cottage, and after a moment's thought, Ivy locked both the front and back door. When she climbed into bed, Beth was lying with her eyes closed, the sheet pulled up to her chin. Resting on the pillow, close to her face, the amethyst glittered in the moonlight.

"Good night," Ivy said softly. "Everything's okay now."

"Don't be fooled," Beth replied. "He's making plans. He wants revenge."

Nineteen

FRIDAY MORNING, BETH AND IVY WERE ASSIGNED TO the garden to weed and deadhead. While Ivy pried at stubborn roots, Beth silently worked her way down the rows of faded blossoms—*snip, snip, snip*. She had spoken little since the morning alarm went off, bringing each conversation Ivy had begun to a quick close with a one-word answer.

"So you don't remember Max coming around, yelling for Dhanya?"

"No."

"Do you remember dreaming?" Ivy asked.

"No."

"Beth, are you mad at me?"

Beth snipped off a flower head that was still blooming. "No."

Ivy gave up.

At three p.m., Aunt Cindy thanked everyone for a solid day's work and shooed them off. Beth, Dhanya, and Will sunned in the garden, the girls falling asleep, and Will finishing up some sketches for *The Angel and the Alley Cat*. Kelsey, deciding she had been much too available to Bryan, headed to Nauset Beach, targeting an area on the long strip of oceanfront that was known to attract surfers.

Ivy returned to Pleasant Bay and handwrote a rambling letter to her mother—Maggie disliked e-mail. Describing Provincetown and recounting funny moments with the inn's guests, Ivy omitted everything of real importance.

That finished, she debated whether to send a text message to her friend Suzanne. She knew that Suzanne's trip to Europe was her way of putting distance between last summer and now. When Suzanne told Ivy and Beth that they wouldn't be hearing from her for a while, Ivy had understood. Suzanne had been totally in love with Gregory, and he had milked that passion as much as he could. Drawing Ivy into his web, he continually strove to make Suzanne jealous. In the end Suzanne, like Ivy, lost someone she truly loved.

Taking out her iPhone, Ivy typed in: MISS U. DON'T HAFTO REPLY. JUST THINKING OF U. LUV IVY. Then she left a voicemail on Guy's phone: "Hi. Hope you're having a good day chopping at tree stumps. Say hello to Fleabag." Finally, she lay back and fell asleep.

Arriving home just before six, Ivy found Dhanya standing in front of the long mirror that was attached to the bathroom door, turning this way and that, studying herself in a short, flirty skirt. "I think I'd better wear my bikini bottom under this," she said, leaning over, looking at herself upside down in the mirror.

"Well, if you're planning to do a lot of that, yeah," Ivy replied, smiling.

Beth emerged from the bathroom combing through her wet hair. She smelled of herbal shampoo.

"Chase called," Dhanya told her.

Beth frowned. "He's been calling my cell all day."

"Well, now he's calling mine. Did you give him my number?"

"No. It's on my phone and I lent it to him to make a call, but . . ." Beth's voice trailed off.

"Anyway," Dhanya said, "I told him you'd phone when you finished your shower."

"You shouldn't have."

"But I thought you'd want to bring him tonight," Dhanya said, and turned to Ivy. "Bryan's uncle gave him passes to his indoor rink, and we're all invited. Want to come?"

"Ice-skating?" It would be awkward with Will, but sooner or later they would have to get used to being around each other. "Okay."

"Awesome!" Dhanya said, and turned to Beth. "The more people we have, the more fun it will be."

"Maybe," Beth said, retreating to the bathroom to dry her hair.

A few minutes later, Kelsey blew in from surfer land, showered, then tugged on thin, skintight biking shorts and a workout top that was more demi-bra than athletic wear.

Chase had earned an invitation on his second call to Dhanya, and Beth's mood shifted from obvious irritation to quiet resignation. As they gathered in front of the cottage, she hung close to Will. Bryan, friendly as always, noticed Kelsey in her sexy outfit, but didn't ignore the other girls. Cracking jokes, he herded everyone toward their cars like a boisterous camp counselor.

Twenty minutes later, they discovered Bryan's Uncle Pat, the rink's owner, had the same outgoing manner.

"Got the date-night music on," he told them as they stood at the counter for skate rentals. "Don't worry, ladies, I didn't pick it out. And Bryan didn't either."

Everyone except Bryan and Max rented skates. Max had ditched his Hawaiian prints for a preppy-looking shirt with jeans; Ivy wondered if word had gotten back to him that Dhanya found him "tacky." Perhaps after driving him home last night, Bryan had given him a little advice.

"I didn't know you were into skating," Kelsey said to Max as he laced up skates that looked expensive and new.

"He's not," Bryan replied for his friend. "Maxie keeps a complete set of toys at each of his residences."

Chase, walking around on his rentals, felt compelled to explain that he had left three kinds of skates at his home in Jackson Hole. Then he turned to Beth and said, "Let me help you with those laces, Elizabeth."

"I've got them," Beth answered, but when she was done, she allowed him to take her hand and lead her to the ice. Bryan and Kelsey followed, then quickly passed them and all the other skaters with their long, athletic strokes.

Max, Dhanya, Ivy, and Will stood awkwardly on the rubber matting. Then Will reached for Dhanya's hand, which left Max and Ivy to feel like the last ones chosen for playground dodge ball.

"Do you want a partner?" Max asked.

"I'd like to skate with you later on," Ivy answered politely, "but I'd prefer to go alone at first."

She skated several circles of the rink, getting lapped by Kelsey and Bryan, but staying behind the couples, enjoying the feel of the smooth ice beneath her feet, and thinking that, if not Bryan's uncle, it must have been her own mother who had picked out the date night music. *Oh, well, anything with a beat.*

When Chase stopped to adjust his laces, Ivy skated up to Beth and linked arms. "I'm snatching your partner, Chase."

Last winter, Beth and Ivy had skated together every weekend, both of them enjoying the exercise. Skating as a pair, matching each other's stride and settling into a comfortable pace, was usually easy for them, but not tonight. Beth skated stiffly.

"I got a text from Philip," Ivy said, hoping Beth's affection for him would serve as a bridge between them.

"So did I."

"I think he misses both of his 'big sisters.'"

Beth nodded.

"He's really looking forward to the newest adventure of *The Angel and the Alley Cat.*"

"Will's sending it Monday," Beth said.

"How's Will doing?" Ivy asked, then felt the jerk in Beth's arm. "Don't pull away from me, Beth. I love him as much as I love you, you know that. Please don't pull away from me."

They skated the curve of the rink, Beth looking straight ahead.

"He's okay," Beth said at last.

"And how are you doing?" Ivy asked.

"Okay."

Ivy felt completely shut out. Striving for patience, she took a deep breath and let it out slowly, watching Max ease back to join Will and Dhanya. There was a moment of conversation, then Max skated off with Dhanya.

Kelsey and Bryan came up from behind and blew past everyone. "I guess you call that power skating," Ivy remarked.

"I'd call it competition," Beth replied. "They compete as a way of seducing each other."

"Compete how?" Ivy asked, glad they had finally gotten a conversation going.

"How much they drink, how long they party, how fast they drive . . ."

"Really! Who told you that?"

"Dhanya. At the beach, they compete to see who can be the most outrageous flirt—with other people, I mean."

"Suzanne and Gregory's old game," Ivy remarked.

Beth met her eyes, then glanced away.

It had been Suzanne and Gregory's favorite sport, and they had played the game like Olympians, an endless competition to see who could flirt and frustrate the other to the point of explosion.

Beth and Ivy skated another lap before Chase caught up, slipping in between them.

"You know, Elizabeth, playing hard to get doesn't always make a guy want you."

"I wasn't playing hard to get or trying to make you want me," Beth replied.

Chase laughed, as if she had meant to be humorous. "I think it's strange—girls dancing with girls, girls skating with girls, waiting for guys to notice them."

"Sometimes," Ivy said, "they're just skating and dancing."

He turned to her, his gray eyes glittering. "Rarely."

He reached for Beth's hand and Ivy watched them skate off, Beth keeping her head turned slightly away. While outwardly compliant, Beth wasn't connecting—not with Chase or me, Ivy thought. The difference was, Chase was so egotistical, he didn't realize it.

She exited the ice, wishing she had brought her own car and could drive home. The rink had a concession area with wooden tables and chairs painted in bright orange and blue. Photos of hockey teams lined the walls. Sitting down, Ivy reached for her phone to see if Guy had called.

"Tired?" Dhanya asked.

Disappointed that there was no message, Ivy glanced up at Dhanya and Max, who had followed her off the ice. "Just taking a break."

"How about an ice cream?" Max suggested. "My treat."

Ivy didn't want any, but she acquiesced, willing to let him score whatever points he could with Dhanya as a "thoughtful" guy.

While they were ordering, Chase, Beth, and Will joined them, so they pushed together two tables and arranged chairs around them. Bryan and Kelsey were the last to leave the ice, staging a rather dramatic conversation—perhaps an argument—in the middle of the rink, which left both of them with flushed cheeks and bright eyes. *Like Suzanne and Gregory*, Ivy thought, as they approached the concession stand. She told herself that it was simply the way some guys and girls played the romance game, but sometimes she felt as if she would never escape the memories of last summer.

The eight of them had just sat down with their ice cream cones when Ivy's phone rang.

Will turned to Ivy as if surprised. Of course, he knew the ring tones of her friends, her mother, Andrew, and Philip, just as she knew the ringtones of his friends and his father. It was one more example of how intertwined their lives had become, that he knew this ring was different. Still, she prickled at the way he looked at her, as if no one should be calling her except the people that he had pre-approved.

Walking a short distance away from the others, she put the phone to her ear.

"Hello?"

"Hey. It's me."

"Hey."

"Whoever that is," Guy added quickly.

Ivy laughed and sat down on a chair at another table. "How was work?"

"Hard. And fun. Guess what, I've got wheels!"

"You do?" Ivy chased a dribble from her ice cream cone, catching it with her tongue.

"Kip has loaned me an old motorbike. So what're you doing?" Guy asked. "That doesn't sound like classical music in the background."

"No. It's disco—good to skate to, I guess." Ivy told him about the rink and free passes. "Want to come over?"

There was a moment of silence. "Who's with you?" he asked.

"Some people you haven't met." Ivy crunched on her cone. "Beth, Max, Bryan, and Chase. And Kelsey and Dhanya, who you might remember from the hospital solarium. And Will. I'd love to see you, Guy."

"I don't think Will would love to."

Ivy glanced over her shoulder. Will and Beth were watching her, and Ivy assumed they had guessed who was calling her. She could ignore their stares and hostility, but it wasn't fair to subject Guy to it.

"Tomorrow then," she said.

They talked a minute more before she returned to the table.

"I can guess who that was," Kelsey teased.

Ivy popped the tip of her cone in her mouth.

"The gorgeous amnesiac."

"The guy they fished out of the ocean?" Bryan asked, his interest piqued.

"In Chatham, right?" Max added. "What was his name?"

"He still doesn't remember," Ivy said. "He calls himself Guy."

"How original," Chase remarked.

"I just don't see how anybody can remain unknown for so long," Bryan said. "Did you Google him?"

Chase leaned forward. "Using what search word?"

"I tried Missing Persons in Massachusetts and Rhode Island," Will told them.

Ivy looked at him with surprise.

"And I assume the police and hospital did the same. I checked again yesterday, but there are still no matches."

"Why didn't you try the FBI's Most Wanted List!" Ivy exclaimed.

"I did. Of course, you have to be already convicted for that."

Ivy turned away.

"I checked with a friend of my father's in New York, a criminal defense attorney."

Ivy swung back. "I can't believe you did that!"

Will continued calmly: "He said that there are major turf battles and little communication between law enforcement officials from one town to the next and across state borders.

Unless a person is running a major drug ring or part of a terrorist group, he could be on the lam or a suspect in a crime, and someone just ten miles away wouldn't be the wiser."

It took all of Ivy's effort not to blow up at him in front of the others. "Thank you for such a thorough investigation, Will." She crumpled the cone's tissue wrapper, and rising, tossed it in a trash can before heading back to the ice.

She had skated half a lap when Bryan caught up with her.

"Contrary to popular opinion, you have a temper," he said, grinning at her.

"Everyone has a point at which they lose their cool," Ivy replied.

"Absolutely," he agreed. "It's one of the interesting things you learn when getting to know a person, the point at which they break. You don't break easily," he added.

Ivy kept skating.

"Is that because you have extreme self-control or because you naïvely believe that people aren't sticking it to you?"

"Are those the only two reasons you see for not losing your temper?"

He skated in front of her, turning to face her, skating backward. "You know another one?"

"Yes. You don't want to hurt the other person."

"Oh, *that* . . ." He smiled at her. "Dance with me, Ivy!"

He slipped around behind her and skated close, his movements precisely matching hers. He faced her again, then turned her so that she skated backward. Like a good dancer, Bryan had both the strength and skill to know how to lean and turn his partner, making it seem easy. Skating with him was fun and Ivy smiled.

Tiring of their dance, Bryan played a pretend game of hockey, rushing ahead, stopping on a dime, spinning back and circling Ivy as close as another skater could without actually touching. He skated backward, then charged her, as if he had a hockey puck, feinting to the left and the right. Ivy grinned and figured she was supposed to keep on skating—that he counted on her to hold a straight and steady line as he weaved and dodged about her. But once he faked so well she couldn't help it: She veered suddenly and they collided.

"Whoa!" He grabbed her to keep her from falling and they spun around, Bryan laughing and holding her tightly. When they stopped spinning, he didn't let go, not right away. Ivy extracted herself from his arms and saw Kelsey watching them.

"Let's just skate," Ivy said quietly to Bryan. "I think you've won this round with Kelsey."

Bryan pulled her hand through the crook of his arm and skated in an easy rhythm with her. "And do you think that is all that I was trying to do—get to Kelsey?"

"Yes."

"Okay, I'll play along with you on that. I can pretend that I am madly in love with Kelsey and see no other girl but Kelsey, not even a girl with incredible hair and green eyes that a guy would never forget."

When Ivy didn't respond, he turned to her. "I fake pretty well, you know."

"I know."

"You saw how well I could feint to the left and right. I can do that in more than hockey."

"Yes, and *you* saw what happens when you fake too convincingly. Not all collisions end well."

Bryan's eyes gleamed, and he threw back his head and laughed. "You have no idea," he said, then skated off.

Twenty

"YOUR BUTLER SHOWED ME IN," IVY SAID TO GUY ON Saturday afternoon, after Fleabag led her along the path that skirted the house to the pond.

Guy smiled and spread a towel beneath the dappled shade of an old apple tree. They sat, resting back on their elbows, and talked about work: the eccentric artist whose lawn full of sculptures Guy had trimmed that morning, and the hermit crab Ivy had found hidden under a child's pillow. Guy's laughter came so much easier now. Ivy savored the sound of it.

"Do you want a swimming lesson today?" she asked.

"I was hoping you had brought your suit."

She nodded. "And a float. I'll be right back."

Ivy changed her clothes in Guy's shed, then cut across the long grass to the pond. A hundred feet from the water she stopped. Guy was nowhere in sight. The cat stood at the pond's sandy edge, staring at the water. Guy's T-shirt lay next to him.

"Oh my God!" Ivy dropped the float and flew down the bank. "Guy!" she shouted. Ten feet into the pond she saw his dark shape at the bottom. "Guy!"

She reached down to pull him up. At the same time he rose to his feet, knocking Ivy backward into the water. Caught by surprise, she came up coughing and sneezing. "What the heck were you doing?"

"What were *you* doing?" he asked back, then, realizing the answer, started grinning. "Oh, you were saving me!"

Feeling foolish, Ivy didn't smile.

"I've been practicing staying under water," Guy explained. "I have to be able to face this fear without my lifeguard hovering over me. Don't be mad, Ivy."

She couldn't be. It was the same thing she had told Tristan the day she had arrived at the pool before him and tested her courage by diving for a penny.

"Look what I found," Guy said, opening his palm.

Ivy's breath caught at the sight of the shiny penny.

"I saw it flashing under the water, like a piece of sun," he told her. "It's a sign."

She looked up quickly. "A sign . . . of what?" *Tristan, are you there?* she asked silently.

Guy hesitated. "Hope. Or maybe it's just a penny."

"No, it's a sign," she told him.

He studied the penny. "Think I'll put this on the blanket. I don't want to lose my piece of hope."

Ivy watched Guy walk to shore, head down, seeming deep in thought as he examined the penny. Should she tell him about that day at the pool when they first kissed? But if Tristan was hiding in Guy and if Lacey was right. . . . "Ready for a swimming lesson?" she asked when he returned, carrying the float.

"As ready as ever."

"Okay. Kicking, breathing, and floating, those are today's objectives," she told him, trying to sound teacher-like and disguise the fact that she felt his eyes wherever they lit on her skin.

She coached him on the flutter kick, then instructed him to use the float and kick his way back and forth across the pond. Their lesson moved on to breathing: "Pretend the water's a pillow for your head," she told him, as Tristan had once told her.

"You're a natural!" she announced ten minutes later.

"You tell that to all your students."

"Let's try the back float," she said, and demonstrated it.

Guy studied her for a long minute, then cocked his head in a flirty way. "Can I just watch?"

"No."

Grinning, he dropped back in the water, seat first, and sank straight down. When he came up sputtering, Ivy laughed, and he splashed her.

"I did the same thing when I was learning. You have to arch your spine and drop your head back far enough so that the water is lapping your forehead."

She showed him again. She remembered how Tristan had placed a hand under her back to support her, then let her go.

I'm floating, she had whispered to him.

You're floating, Tristan had replied, gazing down at her.

Floating . . . Floating . . . Guy was standing over her now and Ivy read it off his lips.

She felt Guy touch the tips of her hair that had spread out in the water behind her. He leaned over her, the sun behind his head making a halo of gold, his face lit by the reflections off the water.

His arms surrounded her and lifted her up. It felt as if her body was awakening from a long sleep.

"Ivy." His mouth formed her name against her throat, then he sought her mouth and kissed her with unbearable sweetness.

The kiss was Tristan's. Ivy knew it, even if Guy did not.

She longed to hold and be held by him. She reveled in the way he brushed her wet hair from her face. When he kissed her ears and the tip of her nose, she laughed at his playfulness, sure that she felt Tristan's joy in Guy's touch.

Tristan, I love you, she thought. *I'll love you always.*

Twenty-one

IVY JOINED BETH AND AUNT CINDY AT CHURCH ON Sunday. With a shorthanded staff, Will told them he would stay at the inn. Through Beth, he had sent a message saying that he was gathering what they needed for the bonfire that evening. *Ever loyal and always thoughtful Will*—was he proving it to her? Ivy chided herself for that thought. He had been through so much with her; he, too, needed this closure.

Maggie and Andrew waited till late afternoon to call, knowing that Ivy would be working most of the day. Now,

with all but two couples checked out of the inn, she had the long front porch to herself and sat alone, gazing at the blue horizon, talking to them on the phone. About ten minutes later, Philip called her from his tree house.

"Lacey visited me this morning," he said.

"She did?"

"In church." Philip giggled. "She started tickling me."

"That sounds like Lacey."

"It was in the middle of Reverend Heap's sermon."

"That *really* sounds like Lacey."

"He gave me a look," Philip went on, "then one of the old ladies who takes care of the flowers started pointing at me and saying 'an angel, an angel!'"

Ivy laughed.

"She could see Lacey's shimmer."

"Then she's a believer," Ivy said.

"But other people, like Reverend Heap, could only see me. Mom turned really red."

"How about Andrew—Dad?" Ivy added, shifting to the name that Philip used.

"He thought it was pretty funny. Anyway, Lacey said she was just checking in because we both missed Tristan. I still miss Tristan."

Ivy got a lump in her throat.

"Mom, Dad, and I looked at pictures of him when we got home."

"Good idea," Ivy said, wiping away a tear. "I think I'll do the same."

After Philip signed off, Ivy stared at her cell phone for a long time, debating whether to call Guy. Today of all days, she wanted to hear his voice.

On the wicker table next to Ivy sat a jug filled with bright pink roses, freshly cut from Aunt Cindy's garden. The scent of them carried Ivy back to the last night she and Tristan had together. He had brought her a bouquet of lavender roses. To Ivy, their unusual color symbolized a once-in-a-lifetime love. And they reminded her of water—water at dawn, water at sunset, the water that gave earthbound Tristan his wings. *Tristan, are you with me?*

It was crazy, she told herself, believing Tristan had come back to her. It was unfair to Guy, seeing someone else in him. And yet, the feeling was so strong. *Tristan, are you there?*

The phone rang. Ivy listened to the ringtone for a full minute before answering. "Hi."

"Hey, it's me," Guy said. "I was afraid you weren't going to pick up."

"I was . . . thinking about things," she said. "What're you doing?"

"Hacking at tree stumps. And you? Besides all that thinking, I mean."

"When the weekenders leave we have a lot of cleanup. I did that and went to church, and talked to my family."

"What's wrong?"

"What do you mean?"

"Your voice," Guy said. "There's something wrong."

Ivy fought back her tears.

"Ivy? Ivy, are you there?" he asked, in response to her long silence.

"Hold on." She dug into her pockets for tissue.

"Are you okay? Ivy, talk to me!"

"I'm okay." She wiped her eyes and blew her nose.

"All right. You don't have to say anything," he told her. "Just don't hang up on me."

"I won't." Finally regaining her composure, Ivy said, "I'm here."

"What's going on?" Guy asked

"Today . . . today is June twenty-fifth."

"Which is a special day," he replied.

Did he know that or was he just guessing? "Yes, Tristan's anniversary," Ivy said aloud. "He died one year ago today."

Guy didn't respond right away. "I'm sorry. What can I do to help? Do you want me to come over? Do you want to come here? Would you rather be alone?"

"Will, Beth, and I are going to have a bonfire at Race Point. Tristan was a terrific swimmer, a racer."

"Then I think he would be happy to be remembered that way."

"Would you come?" she asked suddenly. "Please?"

Guy hesitated. "Um . . . Sure," he said. "I'll meet you there. What time?"

"Around eight."

After their conversation, Ivy went for a long walk. A little after six, she returned to the cottage to change into jeans and found Dhanya sitting on the swing.

"How's it going?" Dhanya asked.

"Okay. Thanks."

"Will told Kelsey and me about the bonfire. He invited us."

Ivy was taken aback. "It's not a party."

"It's a *wake*," Kelsey said, emerging from the cottage carrying a long slice of pizza that flopped over the edge of her paper plate. "And wakes are parties for the dead, the best way to honor the dearly departed."

"His *name* is Tristan," Ivy replied, and headed inside.

She was angry. Why would Will think she'd like to have Dhanya and Kelsey along? But then, she had invited Guy, and Will would be just as unhappy about her invitation. *Be fair*, she told herself.

A half hour later, after Will piled firewood, shovels, and a cooler in the trunk of his car, Ivy climbed in the backseat and Beth in the front. Kelsey and Dhanya followed Will in Kelsey's Jeep. During the thirty-mile trip, Ivy kept waiting for the right moment to tell them that Guy was coming, but couldn't find an opening. Both Beth and Will were quiet. It occurred to Ivy that Will had invited the other girls as a buffer, to keep things from getting too intense.

When the two cars arrived at the parking lot, Kelsey offered to drag the wheeled cooler across the dunes. Will carried the logs and Ivy the kindling. Beth picked up the beach towels and an armful of purple salvia that she had cut from Aunt Cindy's garden. Ivy entrusted Dhanya with the photo album she had brought.

Large dunes separated the lot from the beach and they walked in slow procession along the main path between the dunes. Ivy liked the effort of walking in the deep sand; the ocean breeze was cool, but the sand felt warm beneath her feet.

Ivy and Will dug the fire pit. Beth sat on a beach blanket, holding the album that Dhanya had set down. Kelsey immediately plundered the ice chest, only to discover that no alcohol had been packed. She and Dhanya played in the shallow foam of the ocean, laughing and splashing each other.

When the pit was dug, Will placed the logs and arranged the kindling. Ivy gazed out at the indigo water. Race Point Beach lay along the northern edge of the National Seashore, where the Cape's long finger curled back toward the mainland. The bend in the beach, like the bend in the horizon, made Ivy feel as if she was standing on a ledge between two worlds. The world she had always known was glowing in the west, gold and rose-colored. But another world of mauve and starlight, like the one on the night Tristan had kissed her, hung in the east. She felt caught between.

When the fire was roaring, Kelsey and Dhanya joined the others around it.

"Are we going to sing songs?" Kelsey asked as everyone sat down.

"We're sharing memories of Tristan," Will answered quietly, "talking about the kind of person he was and the things he did."

"That's kind of depressing, isn't it?" Kelsey said, then her face brightened as she looked toward the dunes "Oh, *hello!*"

Everyone turned to follow her gaze. Guy was walking toward them.

"I got here as soon as I could," he said when he was close.

"Who invited you?" Will demanded.

"I did," Ivy replied.

Guy kept his eyes on her. "I brought you some flowers." He held a bouquet wrapped in florist paper behind him, as if uncertain about offering it.

Ivy smiled and stood up, holding out her hands. "Oh!" She looked from the roses to Guy, tears stinging her eyes. "They're lavender."

"I did the wrong thing," Guy said, quickly pulling them away.

Ivy reached for the flowers, her hands catching and holding his. "No! No, they're perfect." She looked into his eyes. "How did you know that—that I love lavender roses?"

He shrugged. "They just seemed right for you."

"They're beautiful. Thank you," Ivy said, cradling the flowers in her arms.

"My parents gave me lavender roses for my sixteenth birthday," Dhanya interjected. "I get a different color each year. And always the number of years I am."

"Before Princess Dhanya tells us the details of each of her very special birthday celebrations," Kelsey said, "grab a soda, Guy. Let's get this wake going."

Ivy made room on her blanket. Guy sat next to her, across from Will and Beth.

Will spoke about Tristan as a top-rated swimmer and Ivy recalled the day Suzanne and Beth had dragged her to her first school meet to watch him compete.

"Can I look at the pictures you brought?" Dhanya asked

Beth passed the album, and Dhanya started turning pages. "Hey, who's this gorgeous guy?" She carried the book over to Ivy, placing it on her lap and squeezing onto the blanket next to her.

"Gregory."

Ivy heard Beth draw in her breath. Will dropped his head and stared at the fire.

"The murderer? Let me see," Kelsey said, scooting

sideways and leaning over them. "He doesn't *look* like a murderer."

"What does a murderer look like?" Beth replied sharply. "How can anyone tell?"

"For one thing," Kelsey said, "there should be cruelty in either his eyes or his mouth. I can't see them in these little pictures."

"Ivy, that's *you*—in that cheesy dress!" Dhanya exclaimed. "Tell me you didn't choose it."

"I didn't. *This* is Tristan," Ivy said, pointing to a photo of a table of wedding guests, which Tristan happened to be passing. Guy leaned closer to study the picture, but she saw no flicker of recognition on his face.

"*The* Tristan?" Dhanya asked. "But he's just a waiter!"

Ivy laughed and told them about her mother's wedding and Tristan's short-lived catering career. "I think it was love at first sight for my little brother, if not for me."

Guy pointed to her brother in another photo. "Philip. I recognize him."

Ivy's heart skipped a beat. Then she remembered they had met at the hospital.

"He's a cute kid," Kelsey said, returning to her own blanket and flopping back to stare up at the darkening sky.

Dhanya turned the page. "Beth, your hair's different. I like it better now."

Dhanya was looking at the picture of Beth, Tristan, and

Ella. "I gave Ella to Tristan," Ivy explained to Guy. "I had to give her up and Tristan answered my ad. He knew nothing about cats, but he assured me he'd take good care of her— said he'd 'wash' and feed her."

Guy smiled. "That was just a ploy to see you."

"Yes. But he soon got attached to her," Ivy replied.

"Where's Ella now?" Guy asked.

"Gregory hanged her," Beth said.

Dhanya gasped. Kelsey let out a low whistle. Will threw a stick in the fire.

"Any which way he could get you," Guy remarked.

"Yes, if it hadn't been for Will, Gregory would have suc-ceeded. Will risked his life for me. He saved me."

Will stared into the flames. Rising to her feet, Ivy went to him. Kneeling close, she put her arms around him. For a minute, he rested back against her, laying his hand over hers.

When Ivy looked up, Guy had shut the album and was watching them from across the bonfire.

Dhanya sniffled loudly.

Kelsey sat up. "Dhanya, you're crying for a cat and a guy you don't even know."

"I know Ivy and Will," Dhanya replied.

"If somebody doesn't get cheerful around here," Kelsey said, "I'm leaving."

No one said anything cheerful.

"All right, boys and girls, I'm out of here. You coming, Dhanya?"

Dhanya shook her head no.

"I'll go with you," Beth said, standing up.

Will and Ivy looked at her surprised.

"It's over. Tristan is gone," Beth told them, tossing her bouquet of salvia into the fire. It flared, flames leaping skyward for a moment, then dropped back. A shower of sparks, darkening to cinders, made Ivy think of falling stars.

"Rest in peace, Tristan," Will said softly.

Twenty-two

WILL AND IVY BURIED THE FIRE AN HOUR LATER. IVY
wished she could ride home on the back of Guy's motorbike, but she could see that Will was still hurting and would
feel betrayed if she didn't return with him and Dhanya.

All of them went to bed early, and Ivy slept solidly
until three a.m., when she was jolted awake. Opening her
eyes, she became instantly alert, as if someone had called
to her. She sat up, listening intently. Beth, Dhanya, and
Kelsey remained asleep. Ivy knelt by the window, pressing her face against the screen, but she neither saw nor

heard anyone outside. Rising to her feet, she slipped on her T-shirt and jeans, then picked up her shoes and wallet, and tiptoed down the steps. Outside the cottage the full moon was high, silvering the garden. Ivy paused only a moment to take in the quiet night, then walked to her car with purpose, as if she had planned hours ago to return to Race Point. She coasted in neutral with her headlights off until she reached the paved road, then flicked them on and drove.

There was a part of Ivy that stood outside herself, wondering at her own actions. This feeling of being called—had it come from a dream? All she knew was that whatever had awakened her, it was something beyond herself.

Ivy left her car in an empty lot at Race Point and walked toward the sea. The rich colors of sunset and bonfire had burned away. The landscape of dune and ocean, bathed in the light of the moon, seemed otherworldly.

"I knew you'd come."

At the sound of Guy's voice, Ivy's heart stopped. Guy had followed her from the path through the dunes. In the moonlight his fair hair was tarnished silver.

"Did you? How?"

"I couldn't sleep, and I kept thinking, *She's going back. I have to be there.*" He stopped six inches from her. "What made you return?" he asked.

"I don't know. I felt like I was being called."

232

They walked together to the fire pit. Ivy had left a single lavender rose on top of the buried fire. Picking it up, she touched its velvet petals with one finger.

"He brought you lavender roses," Guy said.

"You knew that?"

"When I saw the expression on your face, I knew."

Ivy dropped her eyes.

"I was trying to help," Guy told her. "I'm sorry if I made you hurt more."

"You didn't. It felt like—a kind of miracle—getting those roses. It felt like . . . a message from Tristan."

Guy reached for her hand. "Come here. I found a good place to sit." He led her to a sheltered spot between sandy knolls that rustled with beach grass. Sitting on the sand, they rested their backs against a bleached log.

"When you and Will were talking about Tristan," Guy said, "I felt like I knew him."

Ivy gazed into Guy's eyes hopefully.

"How did Tristan die?" he asked.

"Gregory cut his car's brake line," Ivy replied. "We were driving on a winding road, and there was a deer, and another car. We couldn't stop. I lived. Tristan didn't." She searched Guy's face for a flicker of recognition, but he looked away before she could read his eyes.

"Was Gregory jealous of Tristan?" he asked. "Was Gregory in love with you?"

"No, I was the target. I had run into Gregory the night he killed his mother and—"

"His mother!"

"—he thought that I knew he had done it."

"Even so," Guy said, "was Gregory in love with you?"

"For a while he pretended to care. I would wake up from terrible dreams, and he would be there. He was so gentle with me. He would hold me until I went back to sleep."

"So, maybe—"

"No. At the end it was clear—Gregory hated me."

"Love can fuel hate," Guy observed. He drew a triangle in the sand and traced it twice, frowning.

"What is it?" Ivy asked.

He shook his head. "I don't know. Sometimes something seems familiar, and then I lose the thread again."

Ivy reached and smoothed his cheek with the backs of her fingers. "I'm haunted by a past I can't forget, and you're haunted by a past you can't remember."

Guy encircled her with his arms. "So, let's live in the present. Every moment I have with you feels like a gift."

They leaned against the log, gazing up at the stars. His tender kiss became a passionate one. After a while, Guy took off his shirt and spread it on the sand, then lay back on the edge of it, leaving most of the soft fabric for Ivy. She lay down and rested against his chest.

"Sleep, now," he said, holding her securely in his arms. "We're together now. Sleep."

IVY AWOKE TO A SKY STREAKED WITH PEACH AND pink in the east. Guy's arms were still around her, his eyes closed. She slid onto her side and propped herself up on one elbow, studying his face, the golden lashes and rough beard. With one finger she traced the shape of his lips.

His eyes opened. "Good morning," he said softly. "How'd you sleep?"

"Great. I found a good pillow. How about you?"

He raised himself far enough to kiss her shoulder. "I found a sleep mate who doesn't have fleas."

She shoved him down, laughing.

"What time do you have to be at work?" he asked.

"Work!" Ivy sat up and fumbled for her cell phone. It was dead. "Do you know what time it is?"

Guy pulled his phone from his pocket. "A little after five."

"The inn's almost an hour away, and I start work at six thirty!"

"Back to reality," Guy said, rising to his feet, then extending a hand to her. She picked up his shirt and shook it clean.

Guy, who had parked his motorbike by the visitors' center, caught up with Ivy and followed her down Route 6.

By the time they arrived at the Seabright's lot, the sun was shooting yellow rays through gaps in the dark scrub pine. Climbing off his bike, Guy checked his phone again. "Five fifty-eight," he told her.

Ivy leaned against her car, reluctant to say good-bye. "You know, Beth has always said that cars are like clothes—details that develop a story's character."

"And?"

"What kind of car would you like to drive?" she asked.

"Something with a lot of horsepower that looks good with dents."

Ivy grinned. Hand in hand, they walked the path toward the cottage. "What do you think you *did* drive?"

"Probably somebody else's old car. Like my parents' or—I don't even know—" His voice cracked. "I don't even know if I have parents."

"What kind of parents would you want to have? How about a mother who's a doctor?"

Ivy felt Guy pull back. "That's dangerous, Ivy."

"What is?" she asked defensively.

"Imagining things about me. I don't want to get confused. I don't want to mix up what really happened with the things that I want"—he hesitated—"that I want so badly to be true."

What do you want to be true? Ivy was about to ask, then she saw him turn his head toward the cottage.

Beth sat on the swing, Will on the doorstep, both of them with arms folded.

"Where have you been?" Beth asked, her voice hard.

"Race Point," Ivy replied.

"Why did you go back? Why did *he*?"

Ivy bit back anger at Beth's reference to Guy in the third person. "We wanted to."

Will stood up abruptly and strode away without a word. Beth rose from the swing. At the same time Kelsey appeared at the cottage's door, still wearing her satin nightie.

"Well, well, well," she said, holding open the screen door. "Ivy, the good girl, who'd never sneak off on a midnight adventure, returns at dawn." Kelsey winked at Guy. "Looks to me like Ivy had a lot better night than we did."

Beth pushed her way past Kelsey, entering the cottage. Kelsey glanced over her shoulder, then said, "You owe me, Ivy, for not letting Beth run to Aunt Cindy, getting you in a heap of trouble. And you owe me and Dhanya for a lost hour of sleep—Beth was hysterical."

Ivy turned to Guy. "You had better go," she said softly. "Talk to you later, okay?"

He squeezed her hand and silently headed back to the lot.

A half hour later, Ivy was the last one to arrive at the inn's kitchen, dressed for work. It must have been obvious from Will's grim expression, Beth's stiffness, the gleam in Kelsey's eye, and the furtive glances from Dhanya that something had occurred overnight. Aunt Cindy quickly assessed them, and instead of assigning jobs said, "Today I'll need one of you in the garden, one with me for breakfast, one cleaning the room that was vacated late, and two to wash down the porch. Figure it out." Then she left them to make her usual pot of high-powered coffee.

Ivy, wanting to be away from the others, chose the least favorite job, cleaning the room. With work light that morning, all of them finished up early. Ivy headed for the beach below the inn.

She walked halfway down the fifty-two wood steps that descended the bluff and sat for a few minutes on the landing with the benches. She wanted to think about Guy, to remember each sweet moment with him, to run through every sign that Tristan had come back to her. After a while, she descended the remainder of the steps and walked by the water.

Darker thoughts began to creep into her mind. What if Lacey was right, Ivy wondered, and Tristan had done something forbidden when he saved her? If he was hiding inside of Guy, could her loving Guy damn Tristan's soul forever?

At last she returned to the inn and climbed the steps, deep in thought.

"Ivy."

Lifting her head, she saw Beth and Will standing on the landing. Grim-faced, shoulder to shoulder, they made Ivy think of sword-bearing angels forbidding Adam and Eve's return to Eden.

"Excuse me," Ivy said, trying to get past them.

They blocked her way.

"We need to talk," Will said. "Things have gone too far."

Ivy blinked. "What is this, an intervention?"

"Call it whatever you want," he replied. "We're doing it because we care. Ivy, you're not making good decisions."

"You're taking huge risks," Beth said.

"I'm taking the same risk as anyone who has ever loved a person."

Beth shook her head. "But you don't know who Guy is."

"Actually, I believe I know Guy better than he knows himself."

"Which," Will reminded her, "is just what you said about Gregory when his mother was found dead. You felt sorry for him and made excuses for his reckless ways. You said that living with him, you understood him. Now you're making excuses for Guy."

"You're making excuses for a person who can't remember why he was in a fight brutal enough to kill him," Beth added.

"For all you know," Will said, "Guy could have killed someone and been beaten up in the process."

"That's crazy!" Ivy exclaimed. "As crazy as thinking Guy was the driver who ran Beth and me off the road!"

"Ivy, he's pretending he can't remember. Why are you so gullible?" Will cried.

"And why are you so ready to think the worst of someone?" she countered.

"I got an e-mail from Suzanne," Beth said quietly.

"You did?" Ivy leaned against the railing, feeling suddenly worn down by the arguing.

"She's been dreaming about Gregory."

Ivy thought for a moment. "That's not surprising."

"She's been dreaming about him for the last two weeks."

"Beth, all of us have been thinking about Gregory and Tristan for the last two weeks," Ivy pointed out.

"I read the e-mails," Will said. "Suzanne can't remember the dreams—she just knows she's talking to Gregory."

"In the dreams, you mean," Ivy responded. "She's reliving past scenes."

Will clenched his fists with impatience. "I said she can't remember the dreams. But she feels like he is haunting her."

Ivy looked from one to the other. Will's forehead was beaded with perspiration. Beth's fingers pinched her amethyst so hard, their tips had turned bloodless white.

"It was bound to happen," Ivy reasoned. "When Gregory died and the truth came out, Suzanne handled it 'beautifully' as everyone said. But there's no way a person can handle that kind of situation 'beautifully.' It's a nightmare and it will produce nightmares, and it will not go away until it has. There is no shortcut to healing from it. Suzanne is finally doing that now."

"No. Gregory is back," Beth insisted, taking two steps down to Ivy. She laid a cold hand on her arm. "Ivy, you almost lost your life two weeks ago—in a car accident, just like the one Gregory caused last year. What will it take for you to believe me?"

Ivy pulled her arm free and slipped through the gap between her friends. "Your imagination's running away with you, Beth. You and Will have made up your minds, and you're not even trying to listen to me."

"I'm listening," Beth called over her shoulder. "And I hear things that you cannot."

Twenty-three

IT FELT STRANGE, BEING AT ODDS WITH HER TWO best friends. Ivy was worried about Beth, but there was no point in discussing her concerns with Will, not now, when he was convinced that Ivy was the one going off the deep end.

Late that afternoon, having made plans to go with Guy to a summer carnival, Ivy went upstairs to look for something special to wear. She found Beth pacing the bedroom, her cell phone pressed to her ear.

"No, I'm busy," Beth said to the caller. "I've already

made plans for tonight." Listening for a moment, Beth frowned. "I *never* said that, Chase. . . . No, you can't come with me."

Seeing Ivy, Beth turned her back and hunched over the phone.

Ivy watched her for a moment in the mirror, then continued toward her bureau.

"Sorry, I have to go," Beth said, and clicked off the phone.

Ivy glanced over her shoulder. A week ago, she would have sat on the bed, patted the place next to her, and asked her friend, *How's everything?* Now she gazed silently at Beth, who frowned at her image in the mirror, wriggling her shoulders as if she had touched something distasteful, and headed downstairs.

"STRAWBERRY DAYS!" IVY SAID SEVERAL HOURS LATER, happily slipping her hand in Guy's and gazing up at a banner that stretched between two antique fire trucks. The annual weeklong carnival, which raised money for the Cape's fire departments, was a colorful jumble of booths and rides spread beneath strings of lights.

"Where do you want to start?" she asked.

"Games," said Guy, smiling down at her. "I feel lucky tonight. How about darts? Over there."

The booth, tended by a woman wearing a fire hat, had

rows of red, white, and blue balloons. Guy plunked down two dollars.

"Here's your dahts," the woman said with a strong Massachusetts accent. "Good luck."

Guy picked up a dart and turned it in his hands, examining it. "I can't remember . . . which way does it go?" he asked Ivy, then laughed at her reaction. "I'm kidding."

Raising his arm, he aimed and threw. *Pop!*

"One!" said the woman.

He missed with the next dart.

"One for two."

Guy set his jaw and threw—*Pop!*—and threw again. *Pop!*

"Three for four," the woman announced.

Guy threw the final dart. *Pop!*

"Four for five! Pick a prize, any row, sir!"

Guy turned to Ivy. "What would you like?"

"You choose," Ivy told him, curious to see what he would select.

Guy studied the rainbow of stuffed animals. "Top row, third from the left."

The woman handed him a plush white horse with wings.

"It's either an angel horse or Pegasus," Guy told Ivy as he laid the stuffed toy in her hands.

"*Pegasus*," she repeated. "You know your mythology."

Guy gave her a crooked smile. "More proof that I'm a classy guy."

"I always knew it! Thank you," Ivy said, tucking the toy under her arm. "Peg is very sweet."

They moved on to another booth and took turns tossing hoops over bottles, then caught a ride on the Ferris wheel, rising and falling through the twinkling lights of the carnival.

"Want another ride or dinner?" Guy asked her when they got off.

"Dessert for me," Ivy said. "And then another ride. And then another dessert."

He laughed and they walked with arms around each other, following the signs to the food concessions. On the way, Ivy was flagged down by Max.

"Ivy, over here!" he called. He and Beth were sitting on a bench near the bumper cars.

"Who's that?" Guy asked.

"Max. And Beth."

"Is Will here tonight?" Guy's voice held a tinge of uneasiness.

"I think they all came together," she replied, and saw the guarded way Guy glanced around. "Why don't you get in line at the burger stand while I say hello," Ivy suggested.

She joined Max and Beth, squeezing onto the bench. "Hey, where are the others?"

Max pointed. "In the Dodg'ems. Beth didn't want to

drive one. And I know how Bryan and Kelsey get into slamming cars, so I didn't want to either."

Ivy smiled, then stood for a moment to watch. The bumper cars were the old-fashioned kind, with tall black poles ending in snakelike tongues that licked and sparked across a metal ceiling. Will and Dhanya drove smoothly around the polished floor; Bryan, Kelsey, and someone else, spun their cars like lunatics, causing multiple crashes.

"Is that Chase?" Ivy asked, surprised.

"Yes," Max replied, when Beth didn't.

"The smell," Beth murmured. "Ivy, that terrible smell."

"Kind of like burnt hair?" Max asked. "Bumper cars always smell that way."

Ivy sat down. "I didn't think Chase was coming tonight."

"Neither did we," Max replied. "He was waiting in the parking lot and followed us in."

"Be careful," Beth said. "It's dangerous."

Ivy frowned. Was it Chase who was scaring Beth?

"It's electric, but it's safe," Max assured her.

Beth shook her head, twisting the chain of her pendant.

They were carrying on two different conversations, Ivy realized, neither seeming aware that the other didn't understand.

The cars stopped, and Kelsey, Bryan, and Chase kept up their boisterous shoving and laughing as they came down the exit ramp. Will and Dhanya followed quietly.

"Hey, Ivy! You should have been out there with us, you and Guy," Kelsey said, then stopped to look around. "Where *is* Mystery Man?"

Ivy pointed over her shoulder toward the burger stand. "Getting something to eat."

"Mystery Man," Bryan said. "You mean our friendly local amnesiac?"

"Where?" Chase asked, his gray eyes shining with curiosity.

"The gorgeous guy, third in line," Kelsey told them.

They craned their necks to see. When Ivy saw Will's eyes narrow, she turned to look as well.

Guy was talking to a dark-haired girl, shaking his head and gesturing forcefully, as if making a point. He walked away from the girl, but a moment later, after she said something to his back, he turned toward her again and continued the conversation, more heatedly than before.

"Excuse me," Ivy said as she moved toward them.

"Catfight!" Kelsey announced hopefully.

Before Ivy reached Guy, the girl walked away. She was digging in her purse and Ivy caught a snatch of the ringtone from the girl's phone. The girl pressed the phone to her ear, then gazed back one more time at Guy. Ivy barely caught the sound of her light voice as the girl hurried away.

"Did she say '*Bye, Luke*'?" Ivy asked.

Guy spun around. "What?"

"I thought she called you 'Luke,'" Ivy said.

"She didn't," he replied, but he wouldn't meet Ivy's eyes.

"Do you know her, Guy?"

"I've never seen her in my life. She was asking directions."

He had gotten awfully riled up over a set of directions. "To where?"

His eyes sparked. "Is this an interrogation?"

Tilting her head to one side, Ivy studied him. "No."

"Sorry," Guy apologized, his voice softening. "I shouldn't have snapped."

After a moment, Ivy nodded. "And I shouldn't have pressed you."

Guy looked past her, glancing around anxiously. "I'm really tired, Ivy. Do you mind taking me home?"

"Don't you want to eat something?"

"I have stuff in my cooler."

She gave in with a sigh. Perhaps Luke was the name of the person who called the girl on her phone, Ivy thought, as they walked silently to her car. Even so, she knew that something had upset Guy and he was covering it up.

When they arrived back at Willow Pond, Guy didn't want her to stay. "I'm going straight to bed," he said, climbing quickly out of the Beetle.

Ivy opened her door and met him halfway around the

car. "What if I just sit by the pond and check on you in a little while to make sure you're okay?"

"No."

The swiftness of his response made her blink.

"I need some sleep, Ivy. I need . . . some time to myself—some space."

The same thing that she had asked of Will. Ivy's throat tightened.

"I'll be better tomorrow. Don't forget to feed Pegasus," he added with a forced smile.

"Call me," she said.

Without replying, Guy brushed her cheek with the backs of his fingers and walked away.

IVY PACED THE FIRST FLOOR OF THE COTTAGE, mentally replaying the scene between Guy and the girl at the carnival, trying to interpret it. Guy's gestures suggested strong emotions, but whether she had seen anger, frustration, or disbelief, Ivy couldn't say.

If the girl had claimed she knew Guy, why hadn't he told Ivy, so they could pursue whatever clues he now had? Maybe he wanted to check things out without her looking over her shoulder. Maybe he didn't like what he had heard about himself; maybe it was something terrible.

No, Ivy told herself. *Your mind has been poisoned by Beth and Will.*

Still, once suspicion had taken root, she couldn't get rid of it. Each time she passed through the kitchen, she saw Beth's laptop lying open on the table. Was it a desire to help or a failure to trust that tempted her? She wasn't sure, but at eleven fifteen, with the others still out, she sat down to Google the name "Luke."

"Luke" and what? Ivy drummed her fingers. "Luke" and "missing person," she typed, then laughed at herself. Only 51,800 results. She tried "Luke" and "missing person" and "Massachusetts." 8,310 results. As she scanned them she found entries for hospitals named St. Luke and people named Luke who were not from Massachusetts but had a relative there or had passed through there. She could eliminate "St." and "hospital" from the search, but did it really make sense to restrict her search to Massachusetts? Why not Rhode Island or any other state, she thought; Cape Cod was crawling with tourists—the girl at the carnival could have been one.

Perhaps if she searched by date. But when did Guy go missing? The day he was left for dead on the beach, or could it have been some time before? The articles and postings always mentioned age, but she didn't know exactly how old he was.

Ivy continued scanning, clicking on entries, reading description after description of people who had disappeared into thin air. She'd had no idea there were so many.

Had something terrible happened to them, she wondered, or had they "escaped" and lied to start new lives? Engrossed in what she was reading, she didn't hear the footsteps. She wasn't aware of Will until he leaned on the back of her chair.

"Ivy, what are you doing?"

She slammed down the computer lid and whirled around. "Will! You scared me," she said, knowing that was a flimsy excuse for her overreaction.

Will remained unruffled. "Who's Luke?"

When he reached as if he was going to open the laptop, she laid her hand on it. "I don't know."

"Is that Guy's real name?"

"If it is," she replied, "I'm sure you would have discovered that by now with your thorough investigation."

Will grimaced. "I'm not your enemy, Ivy."

"And you think that Guy is?"

He folded his arms. "I think you can't tell the difference between a guy caring about you and a guy using you."

Ivy felt the heat rise in her cheeks. "Get out of here! Get out now!"

Before Will could slam the door behind him, Ivy closed down her search and turned off the computer. If only she could turn off the growing fear in her mind.

Twenty-four

FROM THE MOMENT SHE AWOKE TUESDAY MORNING, Ivy checked her cell phone, but Guy didn't call. It was hard not to phone him, but he'd said he wanted space, so she forced herself to be patient.

Late in the afternoon, finding the phone's silence unbearable, she drove to St. Peter's to practice piano, hoping to fill her head with Chopin, Schubert, and Beethoven. At six thirty, she picked up a sandwich at a café near the church, then returned to practice.

What if something has happened to Guy? she thought,

and almost used that as an excuse to call him. But she knew that Kip had her phone number "in case of emergency" and would have contacted her if there had been a problem. At eight twenty, she drove home, setting her phone on the car seat so she could quickly pick it up.

Arriving at the Seabright, Ivy saw that both Kelsey's and Will's cars were gone. The cottage's windows were dark, and inside it was silent. Ivy walked quietly, reluctant to disturb the building's twilight. In the kitchen only the night-light burned, shining on a note from Aunt Cindy that said she would be out for the evening.

Hoping to take her mind off Guy, Ivy headed upstairs to fetch her paperback mystery. Halfway up the steps she stopped. Candlelight flickered against the bedroom's low ceiling. She tiptoed to the top of the stairs and stared with amazement at Beth, who was sitting on the floor by Dhanya's bed, focusing on the Ouija board. Above the circle of tea lights, Beth's profile was ghostly white, a streak of crimson staining her cheek.

She gave no sign of knowing that Ivy was moving toward her. With her fingers resting on the planchette, Beth closed her eyes and chanted softly. Ivy leaned forward, trying to hear the words.

"*Answer, answer, give me your answer,*" Beth murmured.

Seconds ticked by. Beth's hands, shoulders, and head

were still. The only movement was that of her eyes beneath pale, closed lids. She was like a person dreaming, her eyes darting behind the lids, seeing things that Ivy could not.

"*Answer, answer, give me your answer.*"

The planchette started to move, its motion erratic at first.

"*Answer, answer!*" Beth chanted, her voice more insistent.

The triangular piece moved in a slow circle around the board—counterclockwise. Ivy counted six circles. Then six more, and six more again.

"*Answer, answer, give me your answer. Is it you?*"

The planchette moved to the letter *G*.

Ivy held her breath. *Guy or Gregory?*

The plastic slid sideways and down to the letter *R*.

Ivy watched, nerves tingling.

E . . . G . . . O . . . R . . . Y . . .

"Gregory," Ivy mouthed.

I . . . S . . .

"Is," she said softly, but Beth, deep in a trance, didn't hear.

H . . .

"Stop it!" Ivy cried out.

E . . .

"Stop it, Beth!"

R . . .

"Stop it now!"

Before the planchette touched the final *E,* Ivy leaned down and swept it toward GOOD BYE, then off the board.

Beth's head jerked back as if Ivy had slapped her.

"Beth, what are you doing?" Ivy demanded. "I can't believe you'd try to—"

"He's here" Beth said in a faraway voice. "There's no stopping him now."

A loud knock made Ivy jump. She glanced toward the stairway—someone was at the cottage door. Beth leaned forward and calmly blew out each candle. Before she reached the last, Ivy ran down the steps. Taking a deep breath, she opened the front door.

"Oh, thank God!" she said.

"Ivy, are you okay?" Guy asked and quickly stepped inside. "You're trembling. What's wrong?"

"I'm just—just spooked."

It was too dark to see his eyes, but Ivy could feel Guy studying her.

"Spooked by me?" he asked.

She laughed shakily. "No. Beth—" How could she explain? "It's a long story."

"So let's take a long walk," he said.

"THE THING I LOVE MOST ABOUT BEING ON A BEACH IS that one half of the world is the sky," Ivy told Guy as they stood at the top of the steps that led down the bluff.

"One half of the world is the *stars*," he replied.

Ivy turned to him. *Tristan*, she thought, *do you remember? Do you remember kissing me in a cathedral of stars?*

Guy gazed upward, his head back, taking in the stars. "They're so bright when you're away from town lights. They look closer."

"Close enough to touch," Ivy said.

"There's Orion, the hunter." Guy pointed. "I recognize his sword."

They walked down the steps together, removed their shoes, and followed the path through the dunes.

"Want to walk by the water's edge?" Guy asked. "Now that I know how to float," he added with a smile, "I'm not afraid of drowning in an inch of ocean."

Ivy reached for Guy's hand and they walked toward the water. The tide was receding, leaving behind a cache of silver pebbles and shells. After they had walked a distance, Ivy turned to look at their footprints, his close to hers, matching strides. Guy turned too, then smiled and put his arm around her as they continued to walk.

"So tell me what spooked you," Guy said. "Something about Beth?"

Ivy nodded. "Beth is psychic."

Guy slowed midstride. "She is?"

"Yes, she truly has the gift. But it's a curse, too. What Beth sees, what she senses, often frightens her."

"You said she helped you last year. Did she figure out that Gregory was the killer?"

"She figured out an important part of it."

"What did Beth see tonight?" he asked.

Ivy shrugged off his question. "It doesn't matter. I over-reacted. Sometimes I think that Beth mixes up what she sees and what she imagines. She's got a very fertile imagination."

With one hand, Guy turned Ivy's face toward him and gazed at her steadily. "I think it does matter, because it upset you. But you'll tell me when you're ready." Then he dropped his arm from her shoulder, and said, "Watch this!"

He dashed into the water, up to his thighs, then turned to grin at her, letting a wave race past him. "Are you impressed?" he asked. "Tell me you're impressed."

"Very!"

She ran toward him, kicking up the frothy surf. They held hands facing each other, as wave after wave rushed at them. Each time a wave receded, she felt him gripping her hand harder. "You don't like the undertow."

"It scares me more than a breaking wave," he admitted. "It feels like the ocean wants to pull me back into the darkness."

"I won't let the ocean have you," she said. "Nothing can make me let go."

"How did I ever get this lucky? I must have done something really good in my life."

"You did many good things."

He laughed.

"No, I know it!" she insisted.

Laughing still, he lifted her left hand and kissed her on the knuckle.

"And I believe in something much more than luck," she said.

"Your angels," he guessed. "You've nearly made a believer out of me . . . *Nearly*."

They waded back to shore and followed their own footprints, returning to the path through the dunes. Halfway up the wooden steps, at the landing with the facing benches, Guy reached up and caught Ivy by the elbow. "Can we stop? I want to take a look," he said.

Together they gazed out at the sea and sky, a black and silver eternity.

"I feel like we're floating in midair," he said.

"Halfway between heaven and earth," Ivy replied.

Guy turned to her. Holding her face with both hands, he tilted it up to him, then bent down to kiss her low, in the tender notch of her collarbone. His mouth moved up to her throat, softly pressing against it. "I love you, Ivy."

She rested against him. "And I love you." *Always have,* she said silently.

"I thought I'd lost all that a person can," Guy said. "But I told myself that things couldn't get worse—without an identity, there was nothing left to lose. I was wrong. I'm terrified now that I will lose *you*. If I lose you, Ivy—"

"Hush!" She stroked his cheek with her hand.

"If I lose you, it would have been better to drown."

"You're not going to lose me."

He shook his head. "But if something should come between us—"

"Nothing can," she said. "I promise you, nothing in heaven or earth can come between us."

They turned to climb the rest of the steps and walked slowly around the inn, his arm around her waist, her arm around his. There was no need to speak, no desire to. Ivy didn't want to think about what had occurred in the past or what lay in the future. Tristan had come back to her. To live in the present forever was all that she wanted. All that she had ever wanted was here and now.

"Luke McKenna?"

Startled by the deep voice, Ivy looked up and was surprised to see two police officers. Guy's head jerked around and his arm let go of her.

"You're under arrest," the man said. "You have the right to remain—"

Guy took off, racing for the trees. The officers spun around, flashlights on, but he slipped between the pines and melted into the darkness. The younger officer, a woman, set off in pursuit. The heavyset man stayed with Ivy, arms folded, studying her.

Her mind was reeling. *Luke,* she thought. *His name is Luke.* And he had known it—she had felt him react when the officer spoke his name. How long had he known it—since the carnival? Before?

The police officer turned to glance over his shoulder, and Ivy followed his eyes. Will stood halfway between the cottage and barn.

"Are you aware of how much danger you were in?" the man asked Ivy. "Do you realize what Luke McKenna has done?"

She stared at the officer and said nothing. A cool breeze blew off the ocean, chilling her. "Lucky for you," the officer continued, "that your friend alerted us."

Ivy glanced toward Will, then fixed her eyes on the officer's face. "What is Guy—Luke—being charged with?"

The man's heavy chin and jowls rested against his uniform collar. He was sizing her up, as if he thought she might be faking ignorance. "You have no idea?"

"No," she said, looking him straight in the eye.

"Murder."

Twenty-five

IVY DOUBLED OVER AS IF SHE HAD TAKEN A FIST IN the gut. She could barely walk to the cottage door, and finally reaching it, sank down on the step.

A few minutes later, the female officer returned, winded. "I couldn't catch him," she reported between gasps. "He's in good shape and knows the area better than me. Of course, I could have used some back-up."

The older officer replied, "I didn't hear his bike take off. And we know where he's living. We'll get him." Then he nodded toward Ivy. "I want you to take her in and get a statement. She doesn't *seem* to know anything."

"How old are you?" the woman asked.

"Eighteen," Ivy said, assuming that would keep them from contacting her mother.

"We're not charging you with anything, we just want to ask some questions. Even so, you have a right to have a lawyer present."

"I don't need a lawyer."

"Want to bring your friend along?" the woman suggested, gesturing toward Will, who was approaching them.

Will to the rescue, Ivy thought, *Will to the rescue one more time.* "Thanks. I prefer to go alone."

Will stopped in his tracks.

"Okay, my car's in the lot."

The older officer stayed behind, waiting for assistance in picking up the motorbike. Ivy followed the police car in her Beetle. At the small station she was led to a room that reeked of burnt coffee and the artificial butter of microwave popcorn.

"Can I get you anything—water, coffee, tea?" the police woman asked, pouring herself some muddy coffee, then mixing in dry lumps of creamer.

Ivy shook her head.

"My name's Donovan," the officer said, sitting down at a table across from Ivy. "Rosemary Donovan." She handed Ivy a card with her name, badge number, and phone number, then opened a folder. "I've got some questions."

Slowly, painfully, Ivy answered all of them—how and when she met Luke, how he left the hospital, and what he had told her about his past—nothing. The final question was the most difficult for her: What had she observed about him when she was with him? Ivy stared at the coffee rings on the table between them.

What could she say—that she had observed his kindness toward a stray cat? That when Guy—Luke—kissed her, she nearly wept at his tenderness? How could someone who had seemed so loving be a murderer? How could he have acted so convincingly?

Gregory is here.

Remembering the message from the Ouija board, Ivy went cold all over. Gregory had come back, just as Beth said.

And Lacey was right: Slipping inside Guy's mind, Gregory could easily persuade, tempt.

After a long silence, Donovan asked, "Are you in love with Luke?"

Ivy felt sick. How could she have fallen in love with a heart haunted by Gregory? She dropped her head in her hands.

"Is there something you want to tell me?" the officer asked quietly.

"No."

"Maybe you want to ask some questions," the woman suggested.

Ivy looked up. "Who was killed? Why do you think that"—she hesitated, then made a determined effort to use his real name—"that Luke did it? How did Will know Luke was wanted for murder?"

"Will O'Leary?" Donovan checked the file. "He contacted the hospital in Hyannis, telling them about a patient who had skipped out on them. O'Leary supplied the patient's first name, and the hospital contacted the local police, who contacted other municipalities. A match was made and we realized we were investigating a person who had more than unpaid medical bills on his record.

"As for the victim—" She handed a photograph across the table.

Ivy gazed down at a girl with dark hair and dark eyes, eyes with a spark of mischief in them.

"Her name is Corinne Santori."

"How old?" Ivy asked.

"Nineteen. She was a former girlfriend of Luke's. One friend said they were secretly engaged. She broke it off and he was furious."

"How did he . . . do it?"

"Strangled her."

Ivy shut her eyes, remembering, halfway between heaven and earth, the tenderness with which he had kissed her throat.

"You okay?" the woman asked.

"Yeah." Ivy took a deep breath, then described the girl she had seen him talking to at the carnival. She did not hide the fact that he had lied, denying that the girl had called him Luke.

Lying, denying, and pretending to care, Ivy thought. *Why didn't I see Gregory's presence in Guy?*

When they were done, the officer offered to follow Ivy back to the cottage.

"I'm okay," Ivy insisted.

"Then I'll tell my partner to expect you."

Ivy nodded.

"Be careful, Ivy. Be really careful. We don't want to find another dead girl."

Twenty-six

WHEN IVY ARRIVED BACK AT THE INN, SHE SAW A truck loaded with Luke's motorbike exiting the lot and the older police officer following in his car. Aunt Cindy was still out, but Ivy knew a guest might have spotted the police car and would ask her what had happened. Retrieving a pen and paper from the kitchen, Ivy carried them out to the swing to write a note of explanation. She put down the basic facts: She had learned Guy's name was Luke McKenna and he was wanted by the police; when they'd tried to arrest him, he had fled. The police had questioned her, but she knew nothing about Luke's previous life.

Ivy felt eerily calm as she wrote. It was as if her heart and mind had shut down before they could fully grasp the horror of Luke's actions. She was signing the note when she heard the cottage's screen door open.

Beth stood in the doorway, looking out at Ivy. "How are you doing?"

Beth's voice had its usual sweetness, and the high coloring in her cheeks had disappeared; if Ivy hadn't witnessed the Ouija session earlier in the evening, she wouldn't have guessed it had happened.

"Okay," she replied, figuring that Will had told Beth all the ugly details.

"Do you want to be left alone?"

"No. I'm glad you're here, Beth."

When Ivy showed her the note, Beth rested her hand on Ivy's. "I'm sorry. I'm really sorry."

They were such simple words. Ivy sobbed. The pain was so bad she felt as if she couldn't breathe. Beth laid her hand gently on Ivy's back.

"How could I have been so blind?" Ivy said, choking with tears. "You were right, Beth. You've been right all along. How could I have imagined that Guy was Tristan?"

"I can understand how," Beth replied. "You still miss Tristan. You're still healing. Your heart wanted so much for it to be him, you convinced yourself."

"But you and Will warned me. And I refused to listen. I'm so sorry."

Beth remained silent.

"Lately I've been thinking to myself, *What's wrong with Beth?* But I was the one acting strangely. And you, you could see me making the same mistakes I made before, trusting the wrong person." Ivy took a deep breath and let it out slowly. "It was the night of the séance, wasn't it, when we let Gregory come back into our world?"

Beth nodded, her light hair tumbling forward, shielding her face.

"Last year," Ivy said, "when Tristan came back, it was easy for him to get inside Will's mind. Will wasn't psychic like you, or a believer like Philip, but Tristan got access because he and Will thought alike. In the same way," she reasoned, "it would be easy for Gregory to get inside a murderer's mind."

"Especially someone his age like Luke," Beth replied.

Ivy shuddered. "When you were consulting the Ouija board, the planchette spelled out *Gregory is here.*"

"I thought if I could contact him—" Beth began.

"And when I went down and opened the door," Ivy continued, "there he was."

"He'll be back," Beth said. "At some point, Luke will come back." She grasped Ivy's hand. "Don't pull away from me, Ivy. Not now. We need to take care of each other. Please don't pull away."

Ivy put her arms around Beth. "Never! Not ever again."

———

IVY LEFT AUNT CINDY'S NOTE IN HER IN-BOX. ON HER way back to the cottage she glanced toward the barn. She was still feeling too raw to approach Will and start mending the breach between them. If there was one thing she had learned in the last few weeks, it was that she did not love Will the way she had loved Tristan—with her whole heart and soul—the way she had begun to love Luke. She could not erase that knowledge and pretend that she did.

When Ivy emerged from the shower, Beth was already in bed.

"You okay?" Ivy asked.

"Yes, are you?"

"I'm going to be," Ivy replied with determination.

"As long as we stay together," Beth said, "everything is going to be okay."

Ivy lay awake for a long time, staring up at the cottage ceiling. Beth fell asleep quickly, and Dhanya and Kelsey arrived home an hour later. Ivy remained still until she was certain that everyone was asleep, then rose and tiptoed down the steps. When she turned on the lamp next to the living room sofa, she was greeted with a soft meow.

"Dusty! You're supposed to be out protecting the garden from voles."

The cat rolled on his back for a tummy rub, then leaped off the sofa and strolled to the door. Letting him out, Ivy glanced down at the screen door's broken latch. In a place where the doors were usually kept unlocked, there had been no reason to fix it. For a moment, Ivy considered closing the main door and bolting it, but she retreated to the sofa, leaving it open. Luke was a fugitive from the law and would know better than to show up in a place where others had learned his identity. As for Gregory, bolted doors wouldn't stop him.

Ivy worked on the puzzle, almost finishing it before the urge to sleep caught up with her. She turned off the light. Lying on the sofa, she stared out the screen door to the garden, watching the patterns of moonlight and darkness. Then she rolled over, face to the cushions, and fell asleep.

Sometime later she awoke with a start. Staring at the sofa's striped fabric, Ivy didn't know where she was at first and didn't know what had awakened her. The room was dark, the house still.

Suddenly, a hand clamped over her mouth.

Luke, she thought, and tried to pull the hand away, kicking backward with her legs, but the attacker was strong, his physical power obvious in the little effort it took to control her.

"Ivy, shhh! Shhh!" Luke said.

She fought hard, moving her head from side to side, trying to bite his hand to make him pull it away. *Tristan, help me! Tristan, please!* she prayed.

Luke held her spine tightly against his chest but let go of

her mouth. Before Ivy could scream, he held in front of her a shiny penny. "Ivy, I remember," he said quietly.

"Remember! Remember *what*? Killing Corinne?"

He laid the penny in her palm. "The first time we kissed, you were diving for a penny. I saw you lying at the bottom of the swimming pool and I thought you had drowned. I jumped in after you."

For a moment, Ivy couldn't speak, couldn't breathe.

He laid his palm on top of hers, then twined his fingers around her hand. "They call me Luke, but my name . . . is Tristan."

Her heart pounded the way it had the night of the accident. She turned in his arms, letting the penny slip to the floor. He traced her face lightly with a finger, his own face alight with wonder as he gazed at her. He kissed her, then rested his face against hers. She could feel his warm tears running down her cheeks.

"Tristan, I thought it was you, but then I stopped believing."

"Don't! If you stop believing, there will be nothing but darkness left for me."

She held him tightly. "I love you, Tristan. I will love you always."

"Always, Ivy," he whispered, as he had that night.

"I can't bear to let you go again," she said, and felt the deep breath he took.

"Ivy, something is wrong. I don't know what happened

between the time I said good-bye to you as Tristan and the moment I gained consciousness as Guy—as Luke," he corrected himself, "but something terrible is going on. I feel it in the deepest part of me."

"In your soul?" Ivy asked. "What are you, angel or human? Is it like before, when you spoke through Will and Beth?"

"No." He took a half step back from her and held out his hands. "Luke's face is my face now, his hands are my hands—and only mine. I don't know where Luke's spirit is. His mind and soul aren't in this body, and I have no knowledge of his life beyond what others tell me. The bits and pieces I've been gradually remembering are from my life as Tristan."

"Do you remember Gregory?" she asked. "I mean, more than we talked about the other night?"

"I remember how it was to come face-to-face with him. I remember his gray eyes. Sometimes they were cool and distant, other times, when I caught him off guard, they burned with anger."

"Gregory's back."

"Back?" Tristan repeated. "Ivy, if that's true, you're in danger."

"Earlier tonight, Beth was trying to reach him through a Ouija board. The planchette spelled out *Gregory is here*. And when I went downstairs—" Ivy stopped, a chill going up her spine.

"You opened the door and saw me. Later you found out

that I was accused of murder, and you believed Gregory was in me."

Ivy nodded.

"Who else was in the house then?" he asked.

She didn't answer.

"Ivy, who else?"

She looked over her shoulder, then turned toward the screen door, hearing voices outside. Beams of flashlights swept the garden.

"The police are back," Ivy said, grasping Tristan's arm. "They guessed that you would return. They're looking for you."

Aunt Cindy's voice rose above the others. "This is an inn. I have guests who are sleeping. You cannot come onto private property like this—"

Tristan wrapped his arms around Ivy. "I can't leave you with—"

"They know you only as Luke," she said. "They think you're a murderer. You must go."

"Who else besides Beth was here?" Tristan demanded.

"Come on," Ivy begged, dragging him toward the kitchen door. "Go, Tristan. Please go!"

"You're in too much danger, Ivy."

"You can't help me from jail. Go!"

He pulled her face toward him, kissing her one last time, then slipped out the door.

Ivy knew that if the police found her downstairs, they would guess that he had been there. She hurried up the steps.

"Angels, protect him. Angels, protect me," she prayed.

Then she looked at the bed across from her own. Beth lay sleeping, her face still and pale, her light brown hair feathered out on the pillow. Swallowing hard, Ivy admitted to herself what she had been unable to say aloud to Tristan: the only other person in the house when the Ouija board had spelled out its frightening message was Beth—her best friend, the person she loved like a sister.

Ivy had attributed Beth's headaches to the accident, but thinking back, she realized they had started immediately after the séance. A natural medium, Beth had been the easiest person for Tristan to enter when trying to reach Ivy last summer. Ivy shivered. Perhaps, the night of the séance, Gregory had discovered in her friend's mind the same open portal. Since then, Beth's behavior had grown increasingly strange. Ivy knew what that meant: With each passing moment, Gregory was gaining strength inside Beth.

"Ivy Lyons!" the police called out, pounding on the cottage door.

Ivy almost laughed out loud. Their law and their guns were useless weapons against a demon who wanted only one thing: to destroy Ivy.

Acknowledgments

THANKS TO MY HUSBAND, BOB, WHO ALWAYS LISTENS and makes me laugh; to my sister, Liz, who explored with me her home turf, beautiful Cape Cod; to Karen, who made me so comfortable at The Village Inn; and to Josh Bank, Lanie Davis, and Emilia Rhodes for all their editorial work.